TIM FRAZER
AND THE
SALINGER AFFAIR

Francis Durbridge

WILLIAMS & WHITING

Cover design by Timo Schroeder

9781915887061

Williams & Whiting (Publishers)
15 Chestnut Grove, Hurstpierpoint,
West Sussex, BN6 9SS

Titles by Francis Durbridge published by Williams & Whiting

Also published by Williams & Whiting:
Francis Durbridge : The Complete Guide
By Melvyn Barnes

Titles by Francis Durbridge to be published by Williams & Whiting

Murder On The Continent (Further re-discovered serials and stories)
News of Paul Temple
One Man To Another – a novel
Operation Diplomat
Paul Temple and the Alex Affair
Paul Temple and the Canterbury Case (film script)
Paul Temple and the Conrad Case
Paul Temple and the Geneva Mystery
Paul Temple and the Lawrence Affair
Paul Temple and the Margo Mystery
Paul Temple: Two Plays For Radio Vol 2 (Send For Paul Temple and News of Paul Temple)
The Passenger
Tim Frazer and the Melynfforrest Mystery

INTRODUCTION

Francis Durbridge (1912-98) was the foremost writer of mystery thrillers for BBC radio from the 1930s to the 1960s. As early as 1938 he found the niche in which he was to establish his name, when his radio serial *Send for Paul Temple* was so successful that it resulted in numerous sequels that built an impressive UK and European fanbase. So it was not surprising that Durbridge, while continuing to write for radio, decided to move into television – with the result that in 1952 *The Broken Horseshoe* became the first thriller serial on BBC Television.

The World of Tim Frazer was his ninth television serial, and while the previous eight had each consisted of six thirty-minute episodes this one ran for eighteen thirty-minute episodes covering three stories. Transmitted from 15 November 1960 to 14 March 1961, it was in its time the longest serial ever shown on BBC Television, and it qualified as continuous by using the audience-holding technique of a cliff-hanger ending to each episode but with the changeover in stories taking place during episodes seven and thirteen. Although Durbridge originally planned to use the title *The World of David Marquand*, the change to Tim Frazer cemented the latter's place in television history.

From the first Tim Frazer serial, written jointly with Clive Exton, it was clear that Frazer was a totally different character from radio's Paul Temple - an ordinary man lacking Temple's sophistication, and with no intention of becoming a detective until drawn into the counter-espionage game. The producer/director, Alan Bromly, had been responsible for every Durbridge television serial from *Portrait of Alison* in 1955, and although the other two stories in the Tim Frazer sequence were in the hands of different directors Bromly afterwards returned to direct five more Durbridge serials until *Bat Out of Hell* (1966).

The Durbridge/Bromly partnership consistently provided familiar ingredients - red herrings galore, cliff-hangers ending each episode, and the certainty that viewers should not believe anything that any character says. And consequently Durbridge became recognised as the pre-eminent exponent of the television thriller, the master of the twisting plot following the misfortunes of a protagonist ensnared in a web spun by a killer who remained concealed until the final episode. Indeed the status of Durbridge was rewarded by the BBC, when all his television serials from *The World of Tim Frazer* onwards received the unprecedented accolade of the screen credit "Francis Durbridge Presents" before the title sequence of each episode.

All three inter-linked Tim Frazer serials featured superb performances by Jack Hedley (1929-2021) as Tim and Ralph Michael (1907-94) as his spymaster Charles Ross. While Hedley had appeared regularly on television in the 1950s, his role as Frazer enhanced his reputation and led to film and television successes – including the Hammer films *The Scarlet Blade* (1963) and *The Anniversary* (1968), television's *Colditz* (1972-74) and *Who Pays the Ferryman?* (1977), and the James Bond movie *For Your Eyes Only* (1981). His Durbridge credentials were also to blossom, as he appeared in the Paul Temple television series (*Murder in Munich*, 12 and 19 July 1970) and later was the leading man in the 1983 UK tour of Durbridge's stage play *Nightcap*.

The second Tim Frazer serial, *The Salinger Affair*, was written jointly with Barry Thomas and Charles Hatton, and this time Terence Dudley was the producer/director; while for the third, *The Melynfforest Mystery*, Durbridge was again joined by co-writers Thomas and Hatton but Richmond Harding took over as producer/director. And incidentally, there is widespread disagreement among Durbridge scribes regarding the spelling of Melynfforest – although surely the *Radio Times* can't be wrong?

Durbridge's television serials had the quintessential element of "Britishness", which distinguished them from the numerous American imports then dominating UK television and probably explained his popularity throughout Europe. Already translations of his radio serials had been broadcast in several countries from the late 1930s, and beginning with *The Other Man* (1959 in Germany as *Der Andere*) there were European television versions that attracted a massive body of viewers. In fact Durbridge proved so addictive that German commentators defined his serials as *straßenfeger* (street sweepers), because so many people stayed at home to listen to them on the radio or watch them on television.

In the case of *The World of Tim Frazer*, European television companies produced their translations of the three Frazer serials separately rather than in a continuous sequence. The first was screened in Germany as *Tim Frazer* (14 – 25 January 1963, six episodes), translated by Marianne de Barde and directed by Hans Quest; and the Italian version was *Traffico d'armi nel golfo* (12 – 26 November 1977, three episodes), translated by Franca Cancogni, adapted by Aurelio Chiesa and directed by Leonardo Cortese. The second appeared in Germany as *Tim Frazer – Der Fall Salinger* (10 – 20 January 1964, six episodes), translated by Marianne de Barde and directed by Hans Quest; and in France as *La mort d'un touriste* (3 October – 7 November 1975, six episodes), translated and directed by Abder Isker.

The third Tim Frazer serial became a German television version of particular interest, and not only because of the delay following the two earlier Frazer television translations in Germany. *Das Messer* (30 November – 4 December 1971, three episodes), translated by Marianne de Barde and directed by Rolf von Sydow, was in many ways different from the original - including the re-naming of characters (Tim Frazer became Jim Ellis and Charles Ross became George Baker) and various amendments to the plot with even the revelation of a different guilty party.

The World of Tim Frazer was novelised, but with each of the three serials becoming a separate book. *The World of Tim Frazer* (Hodder & Stoughton, January 1962) was also published in the US in August 1962 by Dodd, Mead. In Germany it appeared as *Tim Frazer*, in France as *Où est passé Harry?* and in the Netherlands as *De wereld van Tim Frazer*. For English-speaking lovers of audiobooks, it was marketed in audiocassettes and CDs read by Clive Mantle (BBC Audio, 2009) and later in CDs there was an abridged reading by Anthony Head (AudioGO, 2010).

The second serial became *Tim Frazer Again* (Hodder & Stoughton, March 1964), published in Germany as *Tim Frazer und der Fall Salinger*, in France *as Le Rendez-vous de sept heures trente* and in Portugal as *O Caso Salinger*. Again audiobook fans were provided with CDs of an abridged reading by Anthony Head (AudioGO, 2011) and a complete reading by Clive Mantle (AudioGO, 2012) as an audio download that does not appear to be available on CDs.

The third serial was much later novelised as *Tim Frazer Gets the Message* (Hodder & Stoughton, November 1978), and in Germany as *Tim Frazer weiß Bescheid*. This time audiobook fans had CDs with an abridged reading by Anthony Head (AudioGO, 2011) and a complete reading by Clive Mantle (AudioGO, 2012).

Melvyn Barnes
Author of *Francis Durbridge: The Complete Guide* (Williams & Whiting, 2018)

This book reproduces Francis Durbridge's original script together with the list of characters and actors of the BBC programme on the dates mentioned, but the eventual broadcast might have edited Durbridge's script in respect of scenes, dialogue and character names.

TIM FRAZER
AND THE
SALINGER AFFAIR

A serial in seven episodes
By FRANCIS DURBRIDGE,
BARRY THOMAS and CHARLES HATTON
Broadcast on BBC Television
27 December 1960 – 7 February 1961
CAST:

Tim Frazer . . . . .Jack Hedley
Charles Ross . . . . .Ralph Michael
Lewis Richards . . . . Francis Matthews
Barbara Day . . . . .Patricia Haines
Martin Cordwell . . . . Donald Stewart
Vivien Gilmore . . . . Patricia Marmont
Det-Insp Trueman . . . . .Victor Brooks
Arthur Fairlee . . . . Michael Aldridge
Hobson . . . . Alan Rolfe
Lloyd . . . . .George Street
Van Dakar . . . . .Anthony Bate
Carol . . . . .Veronica Wells
Detective Sergeant . . . . . . Brian Vaughan
Sue . . . . .Bridget Armstrong
Gordon Dempsey . . . . .Kenneth J. Warren
Leo Salinger . . . . .Hamish Roughead
Waiter . . . . Gertan Klauber
Waiter . . . . Richard Rudd
Barrow boy . . . . .Lee Richardson

Warden . . . . John Gill
Jan .Cameron Hall
Postman . . . . .Anthony Jennett
Porter . . . . Clifford Cox

EPISODE ONE

OPEN TO: The Library at 29 Marsham Square.

TIM FRAZER is holding a folder which is open and contains a photograph of BARBARA DAY, a very attractive woman in her early thirties.
CHARLES ROSS is sitting at his desk, and a shrewd, intelligent looking man – LEWIS RICHARDS – occupies the armchair.

ROSS: (*Indicating the photograph in FRAZER's hand*) Her name is Barbara Day. She's English. Part owner of an antique business. Engaged to a stockbroker named Arthur Fairlee.

FRAZER: And you say she's leaving for Amsterdam on Thursday?

ROSS: Yes.

FRAZER: And you want me to keep an eye on her?

ROSS: Yes.

FRAZER: Why?

ROSS: Just over six weeks ago an agent of ours called Leo Salinger was killed. He was knocked down by a car in Amsterdam. The car was driven by Barbara Day.

FRAZER: And you don't think it was an accident – is that it?

ROSS: (*Looking at RICHARDS*) Well, let's put it this way. Leo was one of our best men. There must have been several people who wanted him out of the way.

FRAZER: But wasn't there an inquest?

ROSS: Oh, yes, there was an inquest. Richards was present; he went over to Holland especially for it.

FRAZER looks at RICHARDS.

FRAZER: (*To RICHARDS*) Well?

3

RICHARDS:	The accident was genuine enough. According to several bystanders Barbara Day tried to pull up, but just didn't have a chance. Salinger stepped right in front of the car.
FRAZER:	(*Nodding*) I see. What was Barbara Day doing in Amsterdam at the time?
ROSS:	She was on holiday.
FRAZER:	And you say she's been back there since the accident?
ROSS:	Yes; she flew over to Amsterdam about three weeks ago. She stayed six days.
FRAZER:	(*To RICHARDS*) And what happened on that occasion? Did you tail her?
RICHARDS:	Yes, I did. I did indeed. (*Dully*) Six days of museums and art galleries.
FRAZER:	(*Smiling*) And yet you're still suspicious?
RICHARDS:	(*Shaking his head*) No, not me. I'm not suspicious. I'm convinced the accident was genuine. These things happen – even to us. (*With a nod towards ROSS*) But Mr Ross here doesn't agree.
ROSS:	All right, Richards. I know you think I've got a bee in my bonnet about Miss Day.
RICHARDS:	Oh, I didn't say that, sir!
ROSS:	(*Smiling*) You didn't have to say it. (*To FRAZER*) Miss Day's taking another trip. She leaves for Amsterdam next Thursday. I want you to tail her, Frazer; find out where she goes – who she meets.
FRAZER nods.	
ROSS:	I'd particularly like to know if she goes to a café called De Kroon.
FRAZER:	De Kroon?

4

ROSS: Yes. It's off the Keizeregracht Platz. Salinger used to go there – quite frequently.

FRAZER: Tell me about Salinger. What was he doing in Holland?

ROSS: He lived there; he worked in Amsterdam. From time to time he supplied us with information.

FRAZER: Did anyone know about this?

ROSS: No; not that we were aware of, although various people must have known that we had a contact in Holland and that information was coming through to us.

FRAZER: What kind of information?

ROSS: Oh, just general information, Frazer – about things in general.

FRAZER looks at ROSS, then at the photograph again.

FRAZER: Of course, Richards may be right. (*Looking up at ROSS*) Perhaps the accident was genuine? Perhaps Miss Day wasn't interested in Salinger …

ROSS: (*Quietly*) Well, that's what I want you to find out.

RICHARDS looks at FRAZER.

RICHARDS: I hope you like museums, Frazer.

FRAZER gives a little smile and looks at the photograph again.

CUT TO:

Inside an aircraft. Day.

BARBARA DAY is seated, looking into the mirror of her compact and powdering her face. Her handbag is on the seat beside her.

MARTIN CORDWELL's voice is heard off screen.

CORDWELL: Thanks a lot, miss.

MARTIN CORDWELL comes into shot and takes his seat behind BARBARA DAY. He is a big, pleasant, tourist type American. He carries a zipper bag with the airways markings on it. There is a cigar case in his breast pocket, full of cigars, and an unlit cigar, in a holder between his teeth.

FRAZER comes into shot, his cine camera strung over his shoulder. He makes to take his seat beside BARBARA, sees the handbag on the seat and hesitates.

BARBARA looks up.

BARBARA: Oh – I'm so sorry.

FRAZER: That's quite all right.

BARBARA takes up the handbag and FRAZER sits beside her.

FRAZER: Thank you. It's pretty warm, isn't it?

BARBARA: Yes, it is.

FRAZER and BARBARA start to fasten their seat belts. Her hand brushes against his in the process. He looks at her. She smiles apologetically. He smiles back at her. She is pleasantly embarrassed.

CUT TO: The Aircraft in flight.

CUT TO: Inside the Aircraft. Day.

MARTIN CORDWELL, the American, is fast asleep. The camera pans to show BARBARA and FRAZER. They have evidently been conversing for some time and are talking now quite freely to each another.

BARBARA: … But you know, it really is extraordinary! Arthur, my fiancé, is exactly the same. As soon as you mention holidays he immediately thinks of the South of France.

FRAZER: Yes, well – I can understand it. The sun's always shining down there and it's a wonderful coast.

BARBARA:	(*Laughing*) Well, I'm sorry, but I prefer Holland.
FRAZER:	Oh, Holland's very nice; it's charming. But the weather's so dreadful, that's the trouble with Holland.
BARBARA:	Oh, nonsense! I've been to Holland several times and had excellent weather.
FRAZER:	Well – you've been lucky, believe me!
BARBARA:	(*Laughing*) I take it this is a business trip of yours, then?
FRAZER:	Well, yes – sort of. I'm an engineer – or rather, I was. I had my own firm. It went bust. Now I'm trying my hand at something I've always wanted to have a crack at.
BARBARA:	Oh, what's that?
FRAZER:	Journalism. I'm going to write one or two articles on Amsterdam.
BARBARA:	Do you think you'll sell them?
FRAZER:	Well, I hope so!
BARBARA:	(*Amused*) Oh, I didn't mean that you wouldn't sell them, I meant …
FRAZER:	(*Smiling*) As a matter of fact I've sold them already. They've been commissioned. They're for a trade paper I used to work for years ago.
BARBARA:	Oh, I see.

The voice of the pilot, CAPTAIN WILLIAMS, is heard over the speaker.

WILLIAMS:	This is Captain Williams, ladies and gentlemen. We shall be landing at Schiphol Airport in approximately fifteen minutes. The weather in Amsterdam is fine and sunny.

BARBARA looks at FRAZER; highly amused.

CUT TO: Schiphol Airport. Amsterdam. Day.
The aircraft is landing.

CUT TO: Amsterdam. Day.
An Amsterdam pleasure boat is arriving at the landing stage near a bridge and the Hotel L'Europe.
Tourists climb out of the launch onto the landing stage. BARBARA DAY is one of them.

CUT TO: The Hotel. Day.
FRAZER is looking in the direction of the landing stage, watching BARBARA. He is holding his cine camera. He holds it up, starting to shoot some film.

CUT TO: The Canal Bridge. Day.
A bridge overlooking one of the attractive canals in Amsterdam.
BARBARA is looking over the parapet at a passing boat.
FRAZER comes into shot, carrying his cine camera.
FRAZER: Good afternoon.
BARBARA turns with a start of surprise. She looks pleased on seeing FRAZER.
BARBARA: Oh – hello there!
FRAZER: Still alone, I see!
BARBARA: Yes, and loving every minute of it! No one to please but myself, for a change.
FRAZER: What are you doing in this part of the town? Don't tell me you've run out of art galleries?
BARBARA: No, I thought I'd take a rest from museums this morning.
FRAZER: (*Smiling*) I don't blame you.
FRAZER stands beside BARBARA, looking down at the water.
BARBARA: It's lovely, isn't it?

FRAZER: Yes. You know, I think you're right about Holland. It's got something. By the way, what do you do with yourself in the evenings?

BARBARA: Oh, nothing very exciting. Find somewhere to eat usually. There's some very nice little restaurants.

FRAZER: Yes, there certainly is. I found a delightful place last night. De Kroon. Do you know it?

BARBARA: De Kroon?

FRAZER: (*Watching BARBARA*) Yes ...

BARBARA: No, I don't. I don't think I've heard of it. Where is it, exactly?

FRAZER: Well, you go into the Dolderplatz and you turn right at Zeeizersgrecht ... No, I'm sorry ... You go into the Keizeregracht and turn right at the Dolderplatz, then you walk through the Middlestrasser and turn left ... No, you don't! You turn left at the Middlestrasser, then when you get to the Keizeregracht ... No, that can't be right ...

BARBARA: (*Laughing*) You obviously haven't the slightest idea where it is!

FRAZER: No, I'm afraid I haven't, but I could take you there. (*A sudden thought*) I say, that's not a bad idea! Why not let me take you there this morning – for a drink?

BARBARA: (*Hesitating*) It's awfully kind of you, but I want to change before lunch because I'm going to ...

FRAZER: (*Interrupting BARBARA*) That's all right! There's loads of time! Meet me back here in an hour.

BARBARA:	Well – (*Suddenly; smiling*) Thank you very much. (*Looks at her watch*) I'll see you back here at twelve o'clock, if that's all right?
FRAZER:	Splendid! (*As she moves away*) Bye now!
BARBARA:	Goodbye!
FRAZER:	And don't be taken in by any strange museums!
BARBARA:	(*Laughing*) I won't …

BARBARA goes. FRAZER looks after her. He shakes his head, thinking to himself that she is evidently quite genuine – there was no reaction from her at the mention of the Café De Kroon.

CUT TO:	The Café De Kroon. Amsterdam. Day.

An open air café-cum-restaurant.

FRAZER is standing taking a movie picture of the surroundings. BARBARA is sitting at one of the tables, watching FRAZER with faint amusement.

FRAZER pans his camera, letting it finally rest on BARBARA. As he does so, the American, MARTIN CORDWELL, comes into shot, joining BARBARA at her table. CORDWELL is carrying a similar cine camera to FRAZER's, also the airway zipper bag. He is smoking a cigar in a cigar holder and looks distinctly tired but nevertheless happy.

CORDWELL:	Hello, there!
BARBARA:	Mr Cordwell!

After a moment FRAZER lowers his camera and goes over to join BARBARA and CORDWELL at the table.

CORDWELL:	What a day I've had! Whew! I've just about walked my feet off buying things to take back home tomorrow.
BARBARA:	(*As Frazer joins them*) Of course – you're flying back to the States tomorrow morning.
CORDWELL:	Uhuh! (*He looks at FRAZER*)

BARBARA: Oh – this is Mr Frazer.

CORDWELL: Glad to know you, sir.

FRAZER takes CORDWELL's hand.

BARBARA: Mr Cordwell's staying at my hotel.

CORDWELL: Yeah, that's right. (*Smiling*) We keep bumping into each other. In boats, buses, cabs, elevators …

FRAZER: Museums?

CORDWELL: No! No! No museums! Not for me! Say, d'you mind if I – er … (*He indicates a chair at the table*)

FRAZER: Of course not.

CORDWELL: I don't wish to intrude if …

FRAZER: No, no, that's quite all right.

CORDWELL plants his zipper bag on the table, puts his camera on the floor, and sits down with a sigh of relief.

CORDWELL: That's better! Europe's a great place, Mr Frazer! I love it. But my feet – will they be glad to get home!

BARBARA laughs; FRAZER places his camera in its case and puts it down on the floor near CORDWELL's, then he sits at the table.

FRAZER: Is this your first visit to Holland, Mr Cordwell?

CORDWELL: No, I was here about five or six weeks ago. Did the whole country in two days – didn't aim to come back but I had rather an unfortunate experience.

FRAZER: Oh – what was that?

CORDWELL: The night I was leaving someone broke into my hotel room and stole my baggage. (*Laughing*) Well, not just the baggage, but everything – literally everything.

BARBARA: Oh, how dreadful for you!

11

CORDWELL: (*Amused*) Yeah! You can imagine – I was in a terrible state! I'd just got the one suit and a sports shirt – the things I stood up in.

FRAZER: What happened?

BARBARA: What did you do?

CORDWELL: Well – I just bought some extra stuff and continued the trip. What else could I do? A week ago the police picked the guy up who did it and sent me a cable. I was in London – just about to fly back to the States – so I came back here.

FRAZER: Did you get any of your things back?

CORDWELL: Yeah, the whole lot – except for a pair of binoculars.

FRAZER: You were lucky.

CORDWELL: I'm glad you think so!

FRAZER: No, no, I didn't mean …

CORDWELL: Sure – sure, I know what you mean, Mr Frazer! (*Laughing*) In a catastrophic sort of way I was kinda lucky. (*Seeing the WAITER close at hand*) Hey, waiter!

The WAITER comes to the table. CORDWELL indicates their glasses, then holds up two fingers to the WAITER.

CORDWELL: The same again! Two! And one for me. (*Three fingers*) Three!

The WAITER nods and goes.

CORDWELL: I bought some cute things this morning, Barbara. Take a look at this.

CORDWELL opens his zipper bag and takes out a model of a Dutchman on a bicycle. The Dutchman is one of those stuffed cloth dolls. He places it on the table and BARBARA and FRAZER view it with amusement and pleasure.

CORDWELL: Now, isn't that something!

BARBARA: (*Amused*) Yes, it's wonderful!

CORDWELL: And here's something else! A real bargain! I bought it just along the street here.

CORDWELL delves into the bag again, takes out a bulb catalogue, puts it on the table, and continues searching in the bag. FRAZER glances at the catalogue.

CORDWELL: That's just a bulb catalogue for my brother. Ah, here we are!

CORDWELL takes a colourful, beautifully designed metronome from the zipper bag and places it on the table.

CORDWELL: It's a metronome! For musicians, you see. Beats out the time. You just wind it up. (*He does so*) Got it for my niece – Shirley. She's quite a piano player – at least, so they tell me. Got no ear for music myself; not the stuff she plays, anyway … There! (*He sets the metronome down on the table and starts it*) There we are! (*He attempts to hum a tune but fails to find one to fit the tempo of the metronome*) Looks great, doesn't it?

BARBARA: It's beautiful …

CORDWELL: Yeah; sure is. I've seen 'em back home, but never one like this.

FRAZER: No, I've never seen one like this before.

CORDWELL: That must be the most God-darned cutest metropole in the world word!

BARBARA: Metronome …

CORDWELL: I beg your pardon – metronome!

They all laugh.

CORDWELL: Shirley certainly ought to go for that; don't you think so, Mr Frazer?

FRAZER: Yes, I do. I do indeed.

CORDWELL: (*Nodding his head*) Sure is a dandy …

CORDWELL sits and looks at the metronome.

CUT TO: London Airport. Day.
An establishing shot.

CUT TO: London Airport – the Arrivals Building. Day.
FRAZER comes out with a PORTER carrying his suitcase.
A car drives up. The DRIVER gets out, takes FRAZER's
suitcase and puts it in the boot. FRAZER gets into the back of
the car and it drives off.

CUT TO: Inside the Car. Day.
FRAZER and ROSS are seated side by side at the back of the
car.

ROSS: … So what it really boils down to is – you agree
           with Richards. You think she is genuine?

FRAZER: Well – yes, I'm afraid I do.

ROSS: You watched her most of the time, I take it?

FRAZER: Yes; I didn't stay at the same hotel but apart
           from that she was never out of my sight. In any
           case, she only slept there; she had most of her
           meals out.

ROSS: What about the café I mentioned – De Kroon?
           Did she go there?

FRAZER: Yes. At my invitation. It was getting near the end
           of our stay and I could see she wasn't going there
           of her own accord, so I thought I'd take her
           along …

ROSS: Why?

FRAZER: I wanted to see if anyone would recognise her –
           the waiters for instance.

ROSS: And did anyone recognise her?

FRAZER: No. (*Suddenly; changing his mind*) Well, that's
           not quite true. There was one man. An American.
           A chap called Cordwell. He was staying at the
           same hotel as Barbara Day. Typical tourist. We

14

	couldn't get rid of him. Went on talking for hours.
ROSS:	About what, exactly?
FRAZER:	Himself mostly. Insisted on showing us his souvenirs. Never stopped complaining about his feet. You know the type ...
ROSS:	Yes.
FRAZER:	(*Reflecting*) There was one thing that made me curious though ... On one occasion he called Barbara Day by her Christian name. Of course, they'd been staying at the same hotel and they'd bumped into one another quite a few times – nevertheless, it was the way he said it. Just for the moment I had the impression they were more than – well – casual acquaintances.

ROSS reflects on this for a moment.

ROSS:	What did this Cordwell look like?
FRAZER:	Oh, he was about forty, I suppose. Pretty tall. Five feet eleven, perhaps ... I've got him on some film I shot at the café.
ROSS:	Has the film been processed?
FRAZER:	No, not yet. (*He takes the film out of his pocket*) It's here.
ROSS:	(*Taking the film*) I'll send it down to the lab. Be at my place this afternoon at three o'clock and we'll take a look at it. (*He leans forward and speaks to the driver*) Drop me off at Orchard Street ...

CUT TO: The Library at 29 Marsham Square. Afternoon.
LEWIS RICHARDS is just finishing threading the film into a projector.
There is a screen on the far wall.
After a moment, ROSS enters carrying a manilla folder.

15

ROSS: Not here yet?

RICHARDS: No.

ROSS looks at his watch.

ROSS: I'm a bit pressed for time. Are you all set?

RICHARDS: Yes …

ROSS: We'll have a look at it and run it again when Frazer arrives.

ROSS moves to the light switch.

HOBSON enters showing in FRAZER.

HOBSON: Mr Frazer, sir.

HOBSON goes.

FRAZER: I'm awfully sorry I'm late. I was held up in the traffic.

ROSS: We haven't shown it yet. You're just in time. (*He indicates a chair*)

FRAZER: Thanks.

FRAZER sits.

ROSS switches off the light, sits next to FRAZER and nods to RICHARDS to start the film.

FRAZER: You'll see Barbara Day herself on the second shot. Getting off the launch after a pleasure cruise.

RICHARDS starts to run the film. They watch the screen.

FRAZER: I shot it from the front of the hotel where I was staying. And there's another one later on, standing on a canal bridge … (*His voice trails away; he looks bewildered as he watches the film*) Wait a minute! This isn't my film!

ROSS looks at FRAZER.

ROSS: What d'you mean?

FRAZER: I didn't take these shots.

ROSS: But you must have done! It's Amsterdam …

16

FRAZER: Maybe, but I didn't take these pictures! (*Indicating the screen*) This building, for instance. I've never even seen it!

ROSS: Richards!

RICHARDS stops the film. ROSS looks back at FRAZER.

ROSS: This is the film you gave me.

FRAZER: But it can't be!

ROSS: (*Irritated*) Damn it, Frazer, I took it down to the lab myself!

FRAZER: (*Quietly; yet firmly*) I'm sorry, this isn't the film I took.

RICHARDS: But it must be!

FRAZER: I tell you it isn't!

ROSS looks at RICHARDS, obviously faintly bewildered.

ROSS: All right. Let's see the rest of it, anyway.

RICHARDS starts the film again.

They watch.

We see the film they are watching.

Various shots of Amsterdam are seen on the screen ending with a shot of a busy thoroughfare.

A man carrying a small parcel is seen walking along the pavement. He is a short, rather distinguished looking man, and appears deep in thought.

ROSS reacts to seeing the man on the screen. He appears to recognise him. He glances fleetingly at RICHARDS who catches his eye. They both look back at the screen with renewed interest.

On the screen the man carrying the parcel steps off the pavement without looking and into the path of an oncoming car.

ROSS and FRAZER react to the man on the screen being knocked down by the car.

On the screen people can be seen rushing to the scene of the accident. The film flickers to a finish.

17

ROSS rises abruptly and switches on the lights.

RICHARDS stops the projector and looks at ROSS. ROSS meets his gaze. RICHARDS, too, has obviously recognised the man in the film.

FRAZER looks bewilderedly from ROSS to RICHARDS, then glances back at the blank screen. Something clicks in his mind. He looks at ROSS who meets his gaze with a slightly blank expression.

FRAZER: That was Barbara Day driving that car!

ROSS: Yes ...

FRAZER: (*Bewildered; indicating the screen*) Then that man – the man that was knocked down – he must have been ...

ROSS: (*Nodding*) It was Leo Salinger. (*Looking at FRAZER*) That was a film of the accident, Mr Frazer ...

FRAZER: But how in heaven's name did that film get ...

RICHARDS: (*Interrupting FRAZER*) Someone must have stolen your film and substituted this one.

FRAZER: But how? And why? I haven't been in close enough contact with anyone for that to happen.

ROSS: What about Miss Day? You've seen her several times?

FRAZER: Yes, but – even if she had this film, why should she want me to see it?

ROSS: (*Faintly irritated*) I don't know why; that's obviously one of the things we've got to find out. Did you arrange to see her again – in London, I mean?

FRAZER: No; I tried to make a date but she wouldn't play.

ROSS: Why not?

18

FRAZER:	(*A shrug*) She's got a fiancé, remember.
ROSS:	(*Crossing to his desk*) Yes; well, I think it's about time you started giving the fiancé a little competition. Bump into her once or twice – casually, of course, you know the sort of thing. Don't play it too hard, or she might get suspicious.
FRAZER:	Yes, all right – but before I start exercising my undoubted charms on Barbara Day, there's something I'd like to know about Leo Salinger.
ROSS:	Well?
FRAZER:	What did he do, exactly? And where was he going when the accident happened?
ROSS:	(*After a moment*) He was a musician. He was on his way to the Academy of Music.
FRAZER:	And what was in the parcel he was carrying?
ROSS:	(*Surprised by the question*) In the parcel?
FRAZER:	Yes.
ROSS:	Why do you ask?
FRAZER:	(*A shrug*) I'm curious, that's all.

ROSS looks at FRAZER, then turns to RICHARDS.

ROSS:	What was in the parcel, Richards?
RICHARDS:	(*Quite simply; a matter of fact*) A metronome …

FRAZER stares at RICHARDS in surprise, then looks across at ROSS.

CUT TO:	FRAZER's Drawing Room. Afternoon.

The room is empty. A telephone on a table is ringing. After some moments FRAZER enters. He is wearing outdoor clothes, having just left ROSS and RICHARDS. He crosses and picks up the telephone receiver.

FRAZER:	Hello? Tim Frazer speaking …

19

BARBARA DAY is heard on the other end of the line. We do not see her during the phone conversation.

BARBARA: This is Barbara Day …

FRAZER: Oh, hello! How are you?

BARBARA: I'm very well, thank you. How are you?

FRAZER: Oh, I'm fine. Did you have a nice trip back?

BARBARA: Yes, I did. Look – I know this is frightfully sudden but I wondered if, by any chance, you'd like to come round for a drink this evening?

FRAZER: Yes, I'd love to.

BARBARA: Arthur Fairlee – my fiancé – will be here. He'd very much like to meet you.

FRAZER: Well – thank you.

BARBARA: Would seven-thirty be all right?

FRAZER: Splendid.

BARBARA: It's twenty-three Crawford House Mansions, near Cheyne Walk, Chelsea.

FRAZER: Twenty-three Crawford House Mansions.

BARBARA: That's right. I'll look forward to seeing you then.

FRAZER: Me too. Goodbye.

There is a click as BARBARA replaces her receiver.

FRAZER stares at the receiver in his hand with a puzzled expression.

CUT TO: Outside BARBARA DAY's Flat in Chelsea. Evening.

FRAZER is ringing the front door bell.

There is no reply.

FRAZER rings again.

He waits a few moments, looks at his watch then rings again, this time holding down the bell push.

The door bell rings with a continued ring.

FRAZER releases the bell push. He is undecided, not knowing whether to wait or go.

He makes to go, changes his mind, deciding to give one last ring.

He rings again.

The door bell rings as before with a continued ring.

FRAZER glances idly down as he stands there.

He reacts to something at his feet.

A Yale key is being pushed under the door from inside the flat.

FRAZER takes his hand from the bell push and stands there transfixed.

Suddenly he stoops and picks up the key.

He looks at the key in his hand, then at the lock.

He hesitates, then tries the key in the lock. It fits.

He turns the key and slowly opens the door. He goes in.

CUT TO: The Hall of BARBARA DAY's Flat. Evening.

FRAZER enters and sees on the rug CORDWELL's Airways zipper bag which is lying half open.

FRAZER stares at the bag and then moves to the living room.

CUT TO: The Living Room of BARBARA DAY's Flat. Evening.

Just inside the door, lying on the carpet, CORDWELL's Dutch doll on the bicycle is torn to shreds. The stuffing is hanging out of it. Near it, on the rug, lies the bulb catalogue.

FRAZER enters, then stops dead in his tracks.

A small table and lamp have been knocked over.

A chair lies on its side and a vase has been broken, suggesting that the room has recently been the scene of a brief struggle.

The body of MARTIN CORDWELL is lying near the overturned table. There is blood on his head and a heavy glass ashtray lies on the carpet near the body.

Not far from the body is CORDWELL's metronome.
The front has been pulled off the instrument and it is lying on its side. But it is still working; ticking away.
FRAZER looks at the metronome, then back at the body.

END OF EPISODE ONE

EPISODE TWO

OPEN TO: The Living Room of BARBARA DAY's Flat. Evening.

Just inside the door, lying on the carpet, CORDWELL's Dutch doll on the bicycle is torn to shreds. The stuffing is hanging out of it. Near it, on the rug, lies the bulb catalogue.

FRAZER enters, then stops dead in his tracks.

A small table and lamp have been knocked over.

A chair lies on its side and a vase has been broken, suggesting that the room has recently been the scene of a brief struggle.

The body of MARTIN CORDWELL is lying near the overturned table. There is blood on his head and a heavy glass ashtray lies on the carpet near the body.

Not far from the body is CORDWELL's metronome.

The front has been pulled off the instrument and it is lying on its side. But it is still working; ticking away.

FRAZER looks at the metronome, then back at the body.

He appears to catch a sound from another part of the flat and listens intently for a moment.

His attention comes back to the body on the floor and he kneels quickly beside it.

He is about to put a hand on the body when the telephone rings.

FRAZER starts, looking across at the small table near the settee where the phone is ringing.

He hesitates, then rises and crosses to the table.

He takes a handkerchief from his pocket, covers his hand with it, and lifts the receiver.

Almost as soon as the receiver is lifted, we hear the voice of VIVIEN GILMORE. It is a quick, business-like voice.

VIVIEN: (*On the other end of the phone*) This is Vivien. I was right, Barbara. He's very curious about Ericson and Lennard Street so I thought I'd better ... Barbara! Barbara, are you there?

FRAZER quickly replaces the receiver and returns his handkerchief to his pocket.

He looks back at the body, kneels down beside it once more and is about to go through the pockets of the dead man – when he freezes, listening intently.

We hear the sound of a key turning in the front door.

FRAZER looks in the direction of the door and rises to his feet.

He looks quickly around and sees the bedroom door.

We hear the sound of the front door closing.

FRAZER goes quickly into the bedroom, leaving the door slightly ajar so that he can see into the room.

BARBARA DAY enters still holding her front door key.

She has evidently seen the zipper bag in the hall and there is an expression of bewilderment on her face.

She does not see the body for a moment, but remains there staring down at the Dutch doll, and the catalogue.

She sees the body and her hands fly to her mouth.

She stares with horror at the body.

She goes slowly towards the body as if, despite her horror, she is drawn to it by some terrible power.

She stops near the metronome, looks at it blankly, then looks again at the body.

Suddenly she turns away, covering her face with her hands.

The telephone rings.

BARBARA uncovers her face, staring blankly in the direction of the phone, then, with a start of relief, she rushes and picks up the receiver.

We hear VIVIEN GILMORE's voice again.

VIVIEN: (*On the other end of the phone*) Barbara! What happened? I was telling you about …

BARBARA:(*With sharp, hysterical force*) Vivien, get off the line! Something dreadful has happened!

BARBARA slams down the receiver and looks quickly across at the body.

BARBARA looks momentarily again at the body before she turns once again to the telephone and takes up the receiver.

The call from VIVIEN GILMORE has pulled her out of her state of shock and passivity and given her the cue for the necessary action in such circumstances.

She starts to dial 999, tremulously repeating the word "Nine" as she dials.

CUT TO: A Block of Flats. Night.
FRAZER is climbing down the last steps of a fire escape which leads down the side of the block.

He runs to his car where it is parked on the corner and drives away.

CUT TO: A Road. Night.
FRAZER's car is driving down the road.

A police car passes it going in the opposite direction, towards BARBARA DAY's flat.

CUT TO: FRAZER's Drawing Room. Night.
LEWIS RICHARDS is sitting in an armchair, a drink in his hand. FRAZER is standing, looking down at him; he is faintly irritated.

RICHARDS: And there are no other rooms in the flat, apart from the bedroom and the living room?

FRAZER: No.

RICHARDS: So whoever murdered Cordwell must have left the flat the same way as you did – by the fire escape?

FRAZER: Yes; after first slipping the key to me under the front door.

27

RICHARDS: M'm. (*He rises and crosses to the drinks table*) Well, they certainly intended you to find the body, didn't they, Frazer?

FRAZER: (*Nodding*) They intended someone to find it. They may not have known it was me.

RICHARDS: But they were expecting you.

FRAZER: Barbara Day was expecting me …

RICHARDS: What do you mean by that? Do you mean you don't think she had anything to do with this?

FRAZER: No; I don't.

RICHARDS: Why not?

FRAZER: I saw her when she entered the flat. She was astonished to find Cordwell there; absolutely amazed. I watched her through the bedroom door. She didn't know what to do. She just stood there – horrified.

RICHARDS: (*Thoughtfully*) Cordwell's bag – the zipper bag – was in the hall?

FRAZER: That's right.

RICHARDS: And the contents of the bag were strewn on the floor near the body?

FRAZER: Yes; it's my bet he was carrying the bag when the murderer attacked him and the contents fell out.

RICHARDS: The contents being: the Dutch doll, the bulb catalogue, and the metronome?

FRAZER: Yes.

RICHARDS: You say the doll was torn – the head was hanging off?

FRAZER: Yes, and in my opinion it had been done deliberately. I think the murderer was looking for something; something which could have been hidden in the doll.

RICHARDS: Yes … (*Looking at FRAZER; a moment*) Tell me about the metronome. What was it like?

FRAZER: Mechanically, it was like any other metronome – but very ornate. Painted up, I suppose, to catch the eye of the tourist.

RICHARDS nods.

FRAZER: Was it Salinger's?

RICHARDS: (*Surprised by the question*) Salinger's?

FRAZER: Yes – the one he was carrying at the time of the accident.

RICHARDS: No.

FRAZER: How do you know?

RICHARDS: We've got Salinger's metronome. It was picked up when the accident happened. It's still in our possession.

FRAZER: Oh, I see.

FRAZER joins RICHARDS at the drinks table.

FRAZER: Well – where do we go from here?

RICHARDS: You don't go anywhere for the moment. You just sit tight and get your story ready for the police.

FRAZER looks at RICHARDS.

RICHARDS: They're bound to ask Barbara Day if she was expecting anyone this evening, and if she's as honest and genuine as you think she is, she'll tell them she was expecting you.

FRAZER: (*Thoughtfully*) Yes …

RICHARDS: But if I was in your shoes, Frazer, I'd beat them to it. I'd ring her now, straight away, and offer an excuse for not turning up.

FRAZER: But supposing the police find out that I did turn up – that I did go to the flat this evening?

RICHARDS: (*With the suggestion of a smile*) Let's worry about that one when it happens.

FRAZER looks at RICHARDS, hesitates, then crosses to the phone.

CUT TO: The Living Room of BARBARA DAY's Flat.
Night.
A tense, somewhat irritated looking BARBARA DAY is sitting on the settee facing DETECTIVE-INSPECTOR TRUEMAN.
The body of CORDWELL has been removed.
In the background we see a photographer packing away his camera and equipment.
A policeman stands near the door.
During the following conversation the photographer nods to the INSPECTOR and goes out.

TRUEMAN: ... I think it's pretty clear, Miss Day, but I'd like to run over your story just once more, if you've no objection.

BARBARA: (*Wearily*) No, I've no objection. Would it matter if I had?

TRUEMAN: (*Ignoring BARBARA's question*) You say you left here at about seven o'clock in answer to an urgent phone call from your fiancé, Mr – er – (*He searches for the name*)

BARBARA: Fairlee. Arthur Fairlee. Yes, that's right. I was expecting Arthur for drinks but he telephoned to say he was ill – he suffers from asthma very badly. He sounded so awful on the phone I decided to go round and see him. He was in a terrible state, poor darling, literally fighting for breath. Finally I gave him a sedative and put him to bed.

TRUEMAN: Then what happened?

BARBARA: I came back here, and that's when I found ... (*She looks quickly at the place on the floor where Cordwell was lying dead*) ... Mr Cordwell ...

TRUEMAN: (*After a moment*) Forgive my asking, but if your fiancé was ill, why didn't you stay with him?

BARBARA: For two reasons. One: I knew from experience that he'd get over the attack, he always does, eventually. Secondly, I'd invited a friend of mine, or rather an acquaintance – a man called Frazer – to meet Arthur and I didn't want him to turn up and find no one here.

TRUEMAN: Did this Mr Frazer turn up?

BARBARA: No, he didn't. Apparently he was delayed in Guildford and couldn't make it. (*She indicates the telephone*) It was Mr Frazer I was talking to when you arrived.

TRUEMAN nods.

TRUEMAN: You described Mr Cordwell as being – just a casual acquaintance.

BARBARA: That's right.

TRUEMAN: How would you describe Mr Frazer?

BARBARA: I'm not sure I know what you mean?

TRUEMAN: Was Mr Frazer just a casual acquaintance too?

BARBARA: Yes, I suppose so ...

TRUEMAN: You suppose so! Was he?

BARBARA: (*Irritated*) Yes, he was.

TRUEMAN: A casual acquaintance – yet you invited him here.

BARBARA: Yes, I did!

TRUEMAN: But you didn't invite Mr Cordwell?

BARBARA: I've already told you I didn't! Anyway, I couldn't have invited him if I'd wanted to.

TRUEMAN: Why not?

31

BARBARA: Because I'd no idea he was in London. I thought he'd returned to America.

TRUEMAN: Did he tell you he was returning to America?

BARBARA: Yes, he did. As a matter of fact I was with Mr Frazer at the time. We were having a drink together at a café and Mr Cordwell suddenly came up to our table. He said he was flying back home the next day.

TRUEMAN: This was in Amsterdam?

BARBARA nods.

TRUEMAN: Did Frazer know Mr Cordwell?

BARBARA: No. So far as I know, they only met that once, at the café. I introduced them.

TRUEMAN: Apart from your fiancé and this Mr Frazer, did you invite anyone else here this evening?

BARBARA: No.

TRUEMAN: (*Looking at BARBARA*) You're quite sure about that?

BARBARA: Yes, I'm quite sure.

TRUEMAN: Thank you.

SERGEANT: Excuse me, sir.

TRUEMAN looks up as a plain-clothes SERGEANT joins them.

TRUEMAN: Yes, Sergeant?

SERGEANT: Just this note, sir.

The SERGEANT hands TRUEMAN a note.

TRUEMAN reads the note, nods to the SERGEANT and puts it in his pocket.

The SERGEANT goes.

TRUEMAN smiles at BARBARA; his first real smile.

TRUEMAN: You've been most helpful, Miss Day.

CUT TO: A Block of Flats. Day.

A taxi stops outside the flats.

FRAZER gets out, pays the driver, and crosses towards the entrance to the flats.

CUT TO: The Living Room of BARBARA DAY's Flat. Day.
BARBARA comes out of the bedroom wearing outdoor clothes.
She looks worried; serious.
She consults her watch, then crossing to the table she picks up the telephone receiver, which is off the hook, and replaces it.
Almost immediately the phone rings.
BARBARA picks up the receiver.
ARTHUR FAIRLEE is on the other end of the line, speaking from his bedroom, propped up in bed.
FAIRLEE is about thirty-five; a stockbroker. He is a chronic asthma sufferer and has developed the habit of pausing for breath now and then whilst speaking, whether it is necessary or not. Although highly-strung and edgy at times, he nevertheless has an air of authority.
During the following conversation we intercut back and forth between BARBARA and FAIRLEE.

FAIRLEE: Barbara, I've just heard the news! I was so stunned I … I … could hardly believe it! Who on earth is this man Cordwell …?

BARBARA: Please, Arthur! Don't get excited!

FAIRLEE: Don't get excited? How can you say that!

BARBARA: Darling, I know this is a pretty awful business, but the very last thing I want is for you to get upset, because it'll only mean …

FAIRLEE: Pretty awful! My God, that's an understatement, if you like! Who was this American? Was he a friend of yours? Because if he was, you never mentioned him!

33

BARBARA: Arthur, listen! Please, listen! I'm expecting
           Vivien. I'll get rid of her as quickly as possible,
           then I'll come and see you. I'll be with you in
           half an hour …
FAIRLEE: Yes, all right …
BARBARA: Now, please, Arthur, don't worry and try not to
           get excited …
FAIRLEE: Half an hour.
BARBARA: Yes, dear …

*BARBARA replaces the phone. As she does so the door bell
rings and she quickly goes out into the hall.*

CUT TO: The Hall of the Flat. Day.

*BARBARA opens the front door and finds FRAZER standing
in the doorway.*

FRAZER: Good morning …
BARBARA: (*Surprised*) Oh – hello …
FRAZER: I hope I'm not disturbing you?
BARBARA: (*Hesitantly*) No, no, I …
FRAZER: May I come in?
BARBARA: Yes. Yes, of course. Please do.

FRAZER enters the hall and BARBARA closes the front door.

FRAZER: I'm sorry to drop in on you like this. I tried to
           ring you …
BARBARA: Yes – I took the phone off. Reporters and
           people kept ringing and I … (*She looks at
           FRAZER*) You've heard, I suppose? You've
           seen this morning's papers?
FRAZER: Not only that, I've had a visit from the police –
           an Inspector Trueman. But why didn't you tell
           me about Cordwell when I phoned you last
           night?

CUT TO: The Living Room of BARBARA DAY's Flat.
Day.

BARBARA enters with FRAZER.

BARBARA: I don't know why, I was in such a state – then
just as you telephoned the Inspector arrived and
… (*Shaking her head*) I can't begin to imagine
what I said to you …

FRAZER: I thought you were angry with me because I
hadn't kept our appointment.

BARBARA: No, no, of course not …

FRAZER: (*With a friendly gesture, touching BARBARA's
arm*) My God, this must have been an awful
shock for you …

BARBARA: I still can't believe it's happened. It's the sort
of thing you read about in the papers, then
when it happens to you …

FRAZER: Yes, I know. When the Inspector told me I was
just … (*He gestures helplessly*) I don't
understand it. What was Cordwell doing here? I
thought he'd gone back to the States?

BARBARA: So did I.

FRAZER: You had no idea that he might be coming to see
you?

BARBARA: No. I still don't know why he came – what he
was doing here.

FRAZER: He didn't mention that he might look you up
some time if he was ever in London?

BARBARA: No, he didn't. Why should he? I hardly knew
the man.

FRAZER: (*Nodding*) That's more or less what I told the
Inspector. Did you see Cordwell again, after
our meeting at the café?

BARBARA: (*After a slight hesitation*) No, I didn't. He must
have left the hotel early the next morning.

35

FRAZER: That's what I thought. (*Suddenly*) Look, I'm sorry if I've dropped in at an awkward moment. I've just realised you've got your coat on. If you're going somewhere perhaps I can drop you?

BARBARA: No, no, that's all right, thank you. I was just going round the corner to see Arthur, my fiancé. He was taken ill last night.

FRAZER: Yes, so the Inspector said.

BARBARA: He suffers from asthma and he had one of his attacks. It was when I got back, after seeing Arthur, that I found Cordwell.

FRAZER: Yes, the Inspector told me.

BARBARA: What else did the Inspector tell you?

FRAZER: (*Hesitantly*) Nothing very much. He just asked me a lot of questions.

BARBARA: (*Curious*) About me?

FRAZER: Well – yes, mostly about you. I had the impression that ... Well, to be honest, Barbara, I think he's under the impression that Cordwell was perhaps a little more than just a casual acquaintance.

BARBARA: Well, he wasn't, I can assure you! (*A pause, then:*) Although I wasn't exactly telling the truth just now when I said I hadn't seen him again after our meeting at De Kroon. He – he came to my room.

FRAZER: When?

BARBARA: That night ...

FRAZER: What happened?

BARBARA: He – made a pass at me. (*A shrug*) Eventually he apologised; said he'd lost his head.

FRAZER: And you didn't see him again?

BARBARA: No, I didn't.

FRAZER: Did you tell the Inspector about this?

BARBARA shakes her head.

FRAZER: Why not?

BARBARA: I didn't think it was all that important, and besides … I thought if I told the Inspector Arthur might very easily get to hear about it.

FRAZER: Would that matter?

The front door bell rings.

BARBARA: Yes, I'm afraid it would. He very quickly gets jealous these days and his asthma makes him quite bad tempered at times. Which isn't surprising, poor darling.

BARBARA turns towards the hall.

BARBARA: Excuse me – that's probably Vivien.

FRAZER: Vivien?

BARBARA: Vivien Gilmore – my partner. We have an antique shop in Islington. Didn't I tell you about it?

BARBARA goes out into the hall.

CUT TO: The Hall.

BARBARA opens the front door and finds TRUEMAN facing her.

TRUEMAN: Good morning, Miss Day. May I come in?

BARBARA: Er – yes. Yes, of course. Please do.

TRUEMAN: (*Entering the hall*) Thank you.

CUT TO: The Living Room.

TRUEMAN enters with BARBARA. He is surprised to see FRAZER.

TRUEMAN: Oh, good morning, Mr Frazer. I didn't expect to see you, sir.

FRAZER: I didn't expect to see you, Inspector.

TRUEMAN: But I'm glad you're here, sir. I was going to phone you anyway.

FRAZER: What can I do for you?

TRUEMAN: I don't know that you can do anything for me, sir – but I would like to ask you and Miss Day one or two questions.

FRAZER: One or two further questions surely, Inspector.

TRUEMAN: (*Smiling*) Yes, perhaps that's a more precise way of putting it, sir. (*To BARBARA*) Miss Day, does the name Ericson mean anything to you?

FRAZER remembers that he has heard the name before and looks across at BARBARA.

BARBARA: No – No, I'm afraid not.

TRUEMAN: Mr Frazer?

FRAZER: Ericson? No – I've never heard the name before. Why do you ask?

TRUEMAN: We found a diary in the dead man's pocket. It indicated that Cordwell had three appointments with a man called Ericson. Today, tomorrow, and the day after.

FRAZER: I see. Did it say where?

TRUEMAN: No. There was nothing but the name – Ericson – written on the dates in question.

FRAZER: Well, I'm sorry we can't help you, Inspector.

TRUEMAN gives a little nod and turns towards BARBARA again.

TRUEMAN: Miss Day – you said you met Mr Cordwell at the café called De Kroon and Mr Frazer was with you at the time.

BARBARA: That's right.

TRUEMAN: Was that the only time you met Mr Cordwell at that particular café?

BARBARA: Yes.

TRUEMAN: You didn't meet him on another occasion, when Mr Frazer wasn't present?

BARBARA: No, I didn't.

TRUEMAN: You're quite sure, Miss Day?

BARBARA: Yes, I'm quite sure! And it isn't the first time I've answered that question, Inspector!

TRUEMAN: What would you say if I was to tell you that you were wrong and that I have proof, definite proof, that you met Mr Cordwell at De Kroon one morning when Mr Frazer was not present?

BARBARA: I would say that you'd either been misinformed or you were trying to be clever!

A pause.

TRUEMAN: Miss Day, we found a film on the dead man. An undeveloped film from a movie camera. Last night the film was processed and early this morning I took a look at it. The film was taken in Amsterdam and apart from some interesting shots of the city – and indeed some very good ones of you, Miss Day – there was a sequence at the Café De Kroon. A sequence in which Mr Cordwell, carrying a zipper bag, was seen joining you – and you alone – at one of the tables. There was, I regret to say, no sign of Mr Frazer.

FRAZER: Of course there wasn't! And for a very good reason! Who the devil do you think took that film, Inspector?

TRUEMAN looks at FRAZER, obviously somewhat taken aback.

TRUEMAN: I don't know, sir. All I know is that we found it on the dead man. Did you take the film, sir?

FRAZER: Yes, I did. And somehow, I don't quite know how, I lost it. Unfortunately I didn't realise I'd lost it until I got home.

TRUEMAN: Then I take it, you've no idea how Mr Cordwell got hold of the film? Or what he intended doing with it?

FRAZER: No, I'm afraid I haven't. I'm just as bewildered as you are, Inspector.

BARBARA: (*Quietly; to TRUEMAN*) You say there were several shots of me, quite apart from the ones taken at the café?

TRUEMAN: Yes. Yes, indeed. Some very nice shots, Miss Day.

BARBARA looks at FRAZER, curious.

BARBARA: Is this true?

FRAZER: Yes.

BARBARA: Well – how did that happen?

FRAZER: (*Vaguely; smiling*) Oh – I saw you once or twice, strolling around, and I thought I'd like to take some pictures of you.

BARBARA: Where did you see me?

FRAZER: Oh – climbing onto boats – getting off boats – getting out of cars – going into museums. (*Pleasantly*) I hope you don't mind. I simply wanted to include you in my memories of Amsterdam.

A pause.
BARBARA is still looking at FRAZER.
It is difficult to tell what she is thinking.

BARBARA: I'm flattered.

CUT TO: Hyde Park. Day.
LEWIS RICHARDS is extinguishing a cigarette in the ashtray of the dashboard of his car. He is in the driving seat. He looks up, seeing someone approaching.
FRAZER walks towards the parked car, opens the door, and gets in.
The car moves off.

CUT TO: Inside the Car. Day.
FRAZER and RICHARDS are seated side by side; RICHARDS driving.
FRAZER looks worried, thoughtful.

RICHARDS: … You still haven't told me why you've changed your mind?

FRAZER: Something happened …

RICHARDS: This morning?

FRAZER: This morning and last night. There was a telephone call from a woman called Vivien Gilmore. She and Barbara Day have an antique business.

RICHARDS: Yes, I know.

FRAZER: It was just after I discovered the body. The phone rang so I picked it up. It was this Gilmore woman. She took it for granted it was Barbara. She said: "I was right, Barbara. He's very curious about Ericson and …"

RICHARDS: (*Interrupting FRAZER; obviously reacting to the name*) Ericson?

FRAZER: Yes. (*Quietly; looking RICHARDS*) You've heard the name before?

RICHARDS: (*Regretting his interruption*) Go on …

FRAZER: She said: "He's very curious about Ericson and …" – then she mentioned some street or other.

RICHARDS: What street?

41

FRAZER: I don't know. I can't remember. Anyway, this morning the Inspector told us that Cordwell knew someone called Ericson – there was a reference to him in his diary.

RICHARDS: And how did Miss Day react to that?

FRAZER: She said she'd never heard of anyone called Ericson.

RICHARDS: And you think she was lying?

FRAZER: If she wasn't, then the phone call from Vivien Gilmore didn't make sense.

RICHARDS: It's a pity you can't remember the name of the street that was mentioned. That might be important.

FRAZER: Yes, I know. I've been trying to think of it ever since I left the flat.

RICHARDS: What did the name sound like?

FRAZER: It sounded like Lombard Street, but it wasn't that, I'm sure. I remember the name Vivien – and the name Ericson – but I'm damned if I can remember the name of the street.

RICHARDS: It'll probably come to you when you're not thinking about it …

FRAZER: Yes, it might. (*Thoughtfully*) Lombard … Leslie … Lennox … (*Shaking his head*) No, that's not it …

CUT TO: A Mews in Knightsbridge.
RICHARDS' car drives up to the outside of FRAZER's flat.
FRAZER gets out, waves to RICHARDS and goes into the building.
The car drives off.

CUT TO: The Front Door of FRAZER's Flat. Day.

FRAZER arrives at his front door and takes his key from his pocket.

He is about to put his key in the lock when he hesitates.

He listens, thinking he has heard something.

He puts the key carefully in the lock, turns it, and slowly opens the door.

He listens again, then quietly enters the hall of the flat.

CUT TO: FRAZER's Drawing Room. Day.

A man's hand is going through papers in a writing bureau. There is a revolver lying near the hands on the bureau.

The man's name is LLOYD. He is a well-dressed man in his late forties. He is not a thug, but looks as if he could be a tough customer if it became necessary.

He puts down the papers with an expression of disappointment and makes to search one of the pigeon-holes.

He freezes on hearing FRAZER's voice.

FRAZER: If it's money you want, I'm afraid you won't find any there.

LLOYD wheels around to face FRAZER who is standing just inside the doorway.

FRAZER: Or is it something else you're looking for?

FRAZER and LLOYD face one another in silence for a brief moment.

FRAZER is angry on discovering the intruder, but he is also curious to know who he is.

He has not seen the gun which lies on the bureau behind LLOYD.

LLOYD is aware of its being there, of course, but does not take it up for the moment.

FRAZER: (*Angrily*) Who are you, anyway?

LLOYD says nothing. He is watching FRAZER closely in case he is armed.

43

FRAZER: All right, my friend!

As FRAZER moves towards the telephone LLOYD grabs the gun from the bureau, levelling it at FRAZER.

LLOYD: Never mind the telephone!

FRAZER freezes.

There is a pause.

FRAZER: (*Quietly*) Who the hell are you?

LLOYD: What's more to the point, Mr Frazer – who the hell are you? And what have you done with them?

FRAZER: (*Genuinely puzzled*) What have I done with them? Done with what? What are you referring to?

LLOYD: (*Irritated*) You know perfectly well what I'm referring to!

FRAZER suddenly springs forward and knocks the gun from LLOYD's hand. It is thrown towards the bedroom door.

LLOYD is taken aback.

FRAZER dives for the gun.

LLOYD goes after him.

FRAZER reaches for the gun, but LLOYD closes with him before he can level it. They struggle on the floor.

After a moment, a hand holding a heavy wooden candlestick comes down into shot.

The candlestick crashes down on the back of FRAZER's neck. He slumps to the floor, unconscious.

LLOYD looks up at the holder of the candlestick.

This is a man called VAN DAKAR who, candlestick in hand, is looking down at the unconscious FRAZER.

VAN DAKAR is a Dutchman, about thirty, cultured, and speaks perfect English.

LLOYD nods his thanks to VAN DAKAR as he rises to his feet.

VAN DAKAR: He's not exactly slow off the mark, is he?

LLOYD: (*Dusting his suit*) No …

VAN DAKAR: I heard voices. I wondered what the devil was going on.

VAN DAKAR nods towards the writing desk.

VAN DAKAR: Any luck?

LLOYD: No. What about the bedroom?

VAN DAKAR: So far – no good. But there's a bureau by the bed. I haven't been through it yet.

LLOYD: I'll take a look at it. Watch Frazer.

VAN DAKAR nods.

LLOYD goes into the bedroom.

VAN DAKAR stands, looking towards the bedroom, then he kneels down by the unconscious FRAZER and goes through his pockets.

He takes out, amongst other things, a wallet and a packet of cigarettes.

He looks at the cigarettes, then after another quick glance towards the bedroom he takes a note from his breast pocket and inserts it amongst the cigarettes, finally closing the packet and returning it to FRAZER's pocket.

He takes up the wallet and is looking through this when LLOYD re-enters.

LLOYD: Any luck?

VAN DAKAR shakes his head.

VAN DAKAR: Just the usual things.

VAN DAKAR returns the wallet to FRAZER's pocket.

VAN DAKAR: I still think you're wrong about him.

LLOYD: (*Doubtfully; looking down at FRAZER*) Maybe … Anyway, we shall see …

FRAZER groans and stirs.

LLOYD indicates with a nod that he and VAN DAKAR go. They move to the door.

LLOYD stops at the radio, switching it on.

VAN DAKAR pauses while LLOYD is doing this, to look back at FRAZER.

He is evidently thinking about the note he left in FRAZER's cigarettes.

LLOYD: (*Indicating the radio*) Drown any noises.

LLOYD looks briefly back at FRAZER and follows VAN DAKAR out.

Slowly, FRAZER comes round and peers stupidly in the direction of the radio.

He opens his eyes and becomes vaguely aware that he is in his own flat.

After a few moments, he sits up, putting a hand to the back of his neck and wincing.

He shakes his head, then rises to his feet.

He goes to the radio and switches it off.

He puts a hand to his head, feeling a little groggy still.

He begins to recollect what has happened when his eye catches the opened bureau.

He ponders over the incident whilst going automatically to the drinks table and pouring himself a drink.

He downs half of the drink and thoughtfully takes out his cigarettes.

He opens the packet to take out a cigarette and sees the note put there by VAN DAKAR.

Puzzled, he takes out the note, opens it, and looks at it.

It reads: "Lennard Street".

FRAZER stares at the note in amazement.

FRAZER: (*Almost inaudibly*) Of course! Lennard Street!

He stares back at the note, obviously wondering how it got into his packet of cigarettes.

CUT TO: Lennard Street. London. N.1. Day.

We see the street sign on this fairly busy street with traffic and shops.

FRAZER is getting out of his car which is parked on a meter.
He looks up and down the street.
He then walks along the street, looking at the shops, etc. and
generally taking everything in.
He does not really know what he is looking for, of course.
He stops, staring across the road. He is looking at a café-
cum-coffee bar called The Amstel.
FRAZER crosses the road and looks in the window of the
coffee bar.
In the window is a model of a Dutch windmill; a model of a
Dutchman riding a bicycle; and a pair of wooden clogs.
FRAZER remains there for a few moments, staring at the
display, then, filled with curiosity, he goes into the place.

CUT TO: The Amstel Coffee Bar. Day.
This is a typical coffee bar with an espresso machine.
There are also tables and chairs.
The motif of the place is essentially Dutch and posters on the
walls show Holland at tulip time.
A faintly harassed WAITRESS is behind the bar, assisted by a
YOUNG GIRL.
The WAITRESS, CAROL, is not usually in charge and is
trying to cope.
One or two people are seated at the bar and at the tables.
FRAZER enters and sits at the bar.
CAROL is serving a man at the counter bar.
The YOUNG GIRL clears some dirty cups from the counter in
front of FRAZER.
GIRL: Yes, sir?
FRAZER: Coffee, please.
The YOUNG GIRL goes to the espresso machine.
FRAZER lights a cigarette and looks discreetly around the
café.
A WOMAN CUSTOMER calls to CAROL.

WOMAN: My bill, Carol, please.

CAROL: Right.

CAROL comes to FRAZER's end of the counter, and starts to make out the bill for the woman.

WOMAN: When are you expecting Jan back?

CAROL: Oh, he should be all right by this afternoon, Miss Gilmore.

FRAZER quickly turns at the mention of the name "Miss Gilmore".

He sees a smartly dressed, faintly masculine woman seated at a table near the bar counter. She is smoking a cigarette.

VIVIEN GILMORE suddenly becomes aware of the fact that FRAZER is looking at her with obvious curiosity, and she, raising her eyes, gives him a long look.

END OF EPISODE TWO

EPISODE THREE

OPEN TO: The Amstel Coffee Bar. Day.

FRAZER and VIVIEN GILMORE are staring at each other. CAROL turns from the counter with VIVIEN's bill and crosses to her table. As VIVIEN takes the bill FRAZER looks away.

VIVIEN: Thank you. What's been the matter with Jan – flu?

CAROL: No – just a tummy upset, that's all. I'll be glad when he's back. There's more than I can cope with on my own here. Specially at lunch times. (*Indicating a young girl*) Sue's all right – but she's a bit on the slow side.

Shooting over FRAZER's shoulder towards where VIVIEN and CAROL are talking, a POSTMAN comes into shots and plants down several letters, one fairly large. He nods to CAROL.

CAROL: Thank you.

POSTMAN: Nice again now.

CAROL: Yes, it is. Not that I've had time to notice it!

The POSTMAN smiles, gives a friendly nod, and goes out. He passes BARBARA, who is just rushing into the café from the street. CAROL has seen her coming, smiles at her, and moves to the counter, taking up the letters and putting them on the shelf under the counter.

BARBARA has reached VIVIEN's table.

VIVIEN: Barbara, I've been waiting here over half an hour! I was beginning to think you weren't coming.

BARBARA: (*Faintly on edge*) I'm sorry, Vivien. I was held up in the traffic. Are you ready?

VIVIEN: Of course I'm ready! I said we'd be there by half-past ten and it's nearly that now.

BARBARA: Well, I'm sorry, Vivien. It just couldn't be helped.

During the above conversation between BARBARA and VIVIEN the YOUNG GIRL has brought FRAZER his coffee and placed it in front of him. FRAZER smiles at her and accepts the sugar bowl as she passes it. He is about to help himself to sugar when, looking up, he suddenly becomes aware of BARBARA's presence. He immediately rises and crosses to her.

FRAZER: Hello, Barbara!

BARBARA: Why, hello! What are you doing in Islington?

FRAZER: There's a firm I used to do business with just down the road. One of our creditors, I regret to say. I'm seeing their accountant at half-past ten. But what about you?

BARBARA: This is our coffee local – in fact I sometimes think we spend more time here than in the shop. Oh – I'm sorry! This is my partner – Vivien Gilmore. (*To VIVIEN*) Tim Frazer. We met in Amsterdam.

VIVIEN: Yes, I remember. You told me.

FRAZER: Nice to meet you, Miss Gilmore.

VIVIEN: (*Unsmiling*) Hello … (*To BARBARA*) Where have you parked the car?

BARBARA: It's on the other side of the road, near the shop.

VIVIEN: I'll see you there, Barbara. Don't be long. Remember the sale starts at eleven o'clock. Goodbye, Mr Frazer.

FRAZER: Goodbye.

VIVIEN goes.

BARBARA: We're off to a sale at Hastings and thanks to Inspector Trueman we're going to be terribly late, I'm afraid.

FRAZER: Trueman?

BARBARA: Yes, I've just left him.

FRAZER:	Then I mustn't keep you.
BARBARA:	No, as a matter of fact, I'm rather glad I've seen you. There's something I'd like to talk to you about.
FRAZER:	What time will you be back from Hastings?
BARBARA:	It's difficult to say. Late this afternoon, I should imagine.
FRAZER:	Well – why not come round to my place this evening, for a drink?
BARBARA:	Thank you. About seven o'clock?
FRAZER:	Yes, that's fine. You've got the address?
BARBARA:	Yes, I have. You gave it to me.
FRAZER:	So I did.

BARBARA hesitates, still looking at FRAZER, then with a "Goodbye, Tim," she goes.

FRAZER looks after her.

A telephone is heard ringing in the background.

FRAZER remembers his coffee at the counter. He goes to the counter and sits, taking up his coffee. CAROL has answered the telephone which is situated in an alcove behind the counter.

| CAROL: | (*On the phone*) I'm very glad, Jan – and relieved to hear it … What's that? … |

FRAZER is still thinking of BARBARA and although he is looking in CAROL's direction he is not taking a great deal of notice of what she is saying.

| CAROL: | (*Still on the phone*) Oh, yes – I've been managing all right except for the lunches. It can be a bit hectic then, as you know … The post? … Yes, he's just been … Just a minute, Jan, and I'll take a look. |

CAROL goes to the counter and taking the letters that the POSTMAN brought from the shelf underneath, she flicks through them. CAROL glances at the YOUNG GIRL behind the counter as she does so.

CAROL: Jan's better. He'll be back this afternoon.

The YOUNG GIRL smiles and hastens to serve a CUSTOMER. CAROL finds the large envelope she is looking for, opens it, and takes out a bulb catalogue.

FRAZER: Could I have my bill, please?

CAROL: Yes – won't be a moment, sir. (*She puts the catalogue down on the counter and returns to the telephone; speaking on the phone*) Hello? … Is it a bulb catalogue, Jan? … Yes – well, it's here … It's just come …

FRAZER hears this speech and quickly turns to stare at the bulb catalogue on the counter.

CUT TO: A street. Day.

This is the street outside The Amstel Coffee Bar.

Shooting along the street, with a barrow and a BARROW BOY in the foreground, the BARROW BOY has his back to the camera at the moment.

FRAZER comes out of The Amstel, looks up and down in search of a telephone box, sees one, and walks briskly towards the camera taking some money from his pocket and examining it as he goes. He stops at the barrow to ask the BARROW BOY for some change. The BARROW BOY is VAN DAKAR, but he appears at this moment to be a perfectly normal barrow boy in dress and manner and is completely unrecognisable to FRAZER.

FRAZER: I wonder if you could change that for me, please? I want to make a phone call.

VAN DAKAR: Sure! Anythin' to oblige! (*He starts to search in his pockets*)

A pause.

FRAZER: (*As VAN DAKAR still searches for change*)
               Well – you'd better give me a pound of
               apples.
VAN DAKAR: (*Briskly*) Thank you very much, Guv.
*VAN DAKAR selects the apples and slips them into a bag. He
hands FRAZER the bag together with his change.*
VAN DAKAR: You'll enjoy those, Guv.
FRAZER: Thank you.
VAN DAKAR: An' if you want to make some easy money
               …
FRAZER: Who doesn't?
VAN DAKAR: "Fantasy" – best tip of the week. It's in the
               two-thirty on Thursday.
FRAZER smiles and turns towards the telephone box.

CUT TO: The Library at 29 Marsham Square. London. Day.
*FRAZER is sitting in the armchair facing an empty desk,
reading a copy of The Times. ROSS comes briskly into the
room carrying a reference book and several documents.
FRAZER puts the paper down and rises.*
ROSS: Sorry to have kept you waiting, Frazer.
               (*Crossing to his desk*) What's the problem?
FRAZER: I told you what the problem was when I
               telephoned you.
ROSS: You said you wanted to see me about
               Richards and Barbara Day.
FRAZER: (*Shaking his head*) I said I wouldn't
               continue to work for you unless you put me
               completely in the picture.
ROSS: You are in the picture. You always have
               been, so far as the Salinger affair is
               concerned.
FRAZER: That's not true, sir, and you know it isn't.
               When I told Richards about the phone call

from Vivien Gilmore and the fact that she'd mentioned the name Ericson I had the impression – the distinct impression – that he'd heard the name Ericson before.

ROSS: (*Non-committally*) It's possible.

FRAZER: Ross, it's no use. You've got to trust me.

A pause.

ROSS hesitates from a moment, then crosses in front of the desk, and joins FRAZER.

ROSS: During the past twelve months Interpol have been very worried about an organisation controlled by a person who calls himself – or herself – Ericson. Ericson deals in diamonds – stolen diamonds – which are smuggled into this country from the Continent, mainly from Holland.

FRAZER: But that's a matter for the police, surely? I don't see what interest your department can have in it?

ROSS: (*Nodding*) We're not interested in the organisation – as such. As you quite rightly say, it's purely a matter for the police. However, there are two angles which involve this department. Some of the diamonds smuggled into the UK have been purchased by foreign agents and it's been our job to supply a list of those agents to Interpol.

FRAZER: But I don't see the connection between this – Barbara Day – and Leo Salinger?

ROSS: (*Nodding*) That's the second angle – Leo Salinger. And to me, at any rate, it's the most important one. Some little time ago I learnt that the Dutch police suspected that

56

Leo was involved in this affair. This news was, to say the least, <u>very</u> disturbing. I trusted Leo implicitly. He'd been working for us for some time and quite obviously possessed a great deal of important information on other matters. If he couldn't be trusted, well ... (*A shrug*) However, apart from that factor I've always prided myself on choosing the right man for the job, so obviously ...

FRAZER: In short: you want to know the truth about Leo Salinger.

ROSS: I've got to know the truth, Frazer! Both for the good of my department and for my own personal satisfaction.

A slight pause.

FRAZER: Was Salinger a friend of yours?

ROSS: (*After a moment*) I'd known him for some time. He and his brother, Arnold, were both at the Academy of Music in Amsterdam. Both brilliant musicians. Their mother was Dutch; their father a British naval officer.

FRAZER: Did Arnold know that his brother was working for your department?

ROSS: No, of course not. (*An afterthought*) Unless Leo wasn't the man I thought he was and the Dutch police were really on to something. In which case, of course he might have told Arnold about our arrangement, or anyone else for that matter. (*A moment*) Well – there it is, Frazer. Now you're completely in the picture. In short: that's all we know.

ROSS returns to his desk.

A pause.

FRAZER: Ross, tell me something. Did you examine the metronome Salinger was carrying?

ROSS: Yes, we did. And we've still got it, of course. It's just a perfectly ordinary metronome. So was the one belonging to Cordwell.

FRAZER nods; he is obviously thinking of something.

FRAZER: What happened to Cordwell's other things – the zip bag, etc?

ROSS: The police have still got them. Why?

FRAZER: Would it be possible to get hold of something for me?

ROSS: Something belonging to Cordwell?

FRAZER: Yes.

ROSS: I don't see why not. What is it you want – the metronome?

FRAZER: No. (*With the suggestion of a smile*) As a matter of fact, I want the bulb catalogue.

ROSS looks quizzically at FRAZER, obviously intrigued by the request.

CUT TO: FRAZER's Drawing Room. Evening.

FRAZER places some cocktail biscuits beside a tray of drinks. He then looks around the room, making sure that everything is in readiness for the arrival of BARBARA DAY.

The door bell rings.

FRAZER goes out into the hall.

CUT TO: The Hall. Evening.

FRAZER opens the front door to find a stranger – ARTHUR FAIRLEE – standing in front of him.

FRAZER: Yes?

FAIRLEE: Mr Frazer?

FRAZER: That's right.

FAIRLEE: My name's Fairlee. Arthur Fairlee. We've never met, Mr Frazer, but I understand that you're a friend of my fiancée's?

FRAZER: (*Not quite sure what to say*) Er – yes. Yes, I am. We met on the plane, going to Holland.

FAIRLEE: So I understand.

An awkward pause.

FRAZER: What can I do for you, Mr Fairlee?

FAIRLEE: It's an awful cheek my dropping in on you like this, and I do apologise. But – I wanted to ask you something and I thought if I just telephoned it might easily give you the wrong … May I come in, Mr Frazer?

FRAZER: Yes! Yes, of course! Forgive me … Do come in!

CUT TO: The Drawing Room.

FAIRLEE enters with FRAZER. He quietly takes stock of the room, noticing the drinks, ice bucket, cocktail biscuits, etc.

FRAZER: Can I offer you a drink?

FAIRLEE: Thank you, no. Are you expecting someone?

FRAZER: Just a friend, that's all.

FAIRLEE: Well, I won't keep you long. It's just that … I'm worried, Frazer! Very worried about Barbara …

FRAZER: Indeed?

FAIRLEE: The police have been questioning me about her relationship with this American chap, Cartwell or Carford – or whatever his name is.

FRAZER: Cordwell. But surely, she's already told them that she hardly knew the man?

FAIRLEE: Yes. Yes, I know, but for some reason or other they … (*Suddenly; getting to the point*) Look, Frazer, as I understand it, you were with

59

	Barbara at that café place in Amsterdam when she met this chap?
FRAZER:	Yes.
FAIRLEE:	(*Hesitantly*) Well – did <u>you</u> get the impression that they might, perhaps, have met before somewhere?
FRAZER:	Met before? No, I don't think so. (*Curious*) Is that why you came here this evening – to ask me that question?
FAIRLEE:	(*Faintly embarrassed*) Er – well – to be honest, yes.
FRAZER:	Well, it all depends what you mean by "met before", of course. They'd seen each other before and passed the time of day. They were staying at the same hotel.
FAIRLEE:	Oh, yes – yes, I know. I didn't mean that, I meant …
FRAZER:	What did you mean?
FAIRLEE:	Well, I meant, do you think they'd been particularly friendly at any time?
FRAZER:	No, I don't. But then, I don't know your fiancée as well as you do, Mr Fairlee.
FAIRLEE:	Oh, please – for heaven's sake, don't go and get the wrong impression about Barbara! I shouldn't have given this matter a moment's thought if it hadn't been for the police. But they've been asking such a devil of a lot of questions – they really have! Believe it or not, they've even questioned Vivien Gilmore.
FRAZER:	Why Miss Gilmore?
FAIRLEE:	I don't know why. Haven't the slightest idea, old man. I suppose it's because she and Barbara are in business together. They have an antique shop in Islington.

FRAZER: Yes, I know. Does Miss Gilmore spend her holidays in Holland?

FAIRLEE: (*Surprised by the question*) No, as a matter of fact she hates the place. Why do you ask?

FRAZER: Well, I thought perhaps that's why they'd questioned her …

FAIRLEE: Oh, I see. No, Vivien can't stand Holland. And frankly, old man, I agree with her. Damn dull hole, if you ask me. (*Shaking his head*) And why Barbara should want to go back there after that terrible accident, just beats me.

FRAZER: Accident?

FAIRLEE: Yes, didn't she tell you about it?

FRAZER: No. What accident?

FAIRLEE: (*Watching FRAZER as he speaks*) She ran over a man in Amsterdam – a chap called Salinger. The poor devil was killed.

FRAZER: Good heavens! What a dreadful experience!

FAIRLEE: Yes, nasty business, nasty business altogether. Still, it wasn't her fault, thank God. (*Suddenly*) I must go! Thank you, Frazer, for being so tolerant, and my apologies again for coming in on the hop like this.

FRAZER: Not at all.

FAIRLEE: Oh – and by the way, I'd be grateful if you'd … Well, please don't say anything to Barbara about my visit. I wouldn't like her to think I was checking up on her, as it were.

FRAZER nods, obviously thinking that this is precisely what ARTHUR FAIRLEE has been doing.

The door bell rings.

FRAZER looks towards the hall, and hesitates.

FAIRLEE: That's your friend. I'll be off.

FRAZER indicates to ARTHUR to precede him into the hall. FAIRLEE goes into the hall and FRAZER follows him, somewhat anxiously.

CUT TO: The Hall
FAIRLEE comes into the hall and stands there while FRAZER goes to the front door to open it.
FRAZER is thinking rapidly – ready to feign surprise at BARBARA's being there.
FRAZER opens the front door.
LEWIS RICHARDS is standing in the doorway. FRAZER is obviously relieved.
RICHARDS: Good evening. (*He looks quickly at FAIRLEE*)
FRAZER immediately pretends that this is the "friend" he was expecting.
FRAZER: Ah – I was beginning to wonder whether you
            were coming or not.
RICHARDS registers slight surprise at this, but conceals it with professional skill. He looks again at ARTHUR FAIRLEE.
FRAZER: Oh – this is Arthur Fairlee. George Richards …
There is a fleeting reaction to the "George" from RICHARDS.
RICHARDS: (*To FAIRLEE*) How do you do?
FAIRLEE: How do you do? (*To FRAZER*) Well, I'll be
            going. You won't say anything about …?
FRAZER: (*Shaking his head*) No, I won't. Goodbye.
FAIRLEE: Goodbye.
FAIRLEE nods to RICHARDS and goes. FRAZER closes the front door and indicates to RICHARDS to go into the drawing room.

CUT TO: The Drawing Room
RICHARDS enters, followed by FRAZER.
RICHARDS: It's not "George", by the way – it's Lewis.

FRAZER: (*Smiling*) I told him I had a friend coming. "Mr Richards" doesn't sound exactly friendly.

RICHARDS is looking at the drinks and biscuits.

RICHARDS: And the "friend" presumably is Barbara Day?

Their eyes hold for a moment.

FRAZER: What will you have to drink?

RICHARDS: Whisky, please.

FRAZER goes to the drinks table and mixes some drinks.
RICHARDS watches him.

RICHARDS: What did Fairlee want?

FRAZER: I'm not sure. (*Thoughtfully*) It could be the jealous fiancé routine – but I'm not really sure.

FRAZER gives RICHARDS his drink; sees RICHARDS is studying him closely.

RICHARDS: Skoal!

They raise their glasses and drink.

RICHARDS: I hear you had a chat with Ross this afternoon?

FRAZER: Yes. It cleared the air, if nothing else.

RICHARDS: I understand you asked for the bulb catalogue which belonged to Cordwell.

FRAZER: That's right.

RICHARDS: Ross didn't say why you wanted it …

FRAZER: I didn't tell him why. He didn't ask, for one thing, and even if he had I couldn't have told him. (*With a shrug*) It's just a hunch I have.

RICHARDS gives a little smile and nods.

RICHARDS: By the way, the film they found on Cordwell's body …

FRAZER: My film?

RICHARDS: Yes. Miss Day asked Inspector Trueman if she could take a look at it. They ran it through for her this morning.

FRAZER: (*Puzzled*) Did she give you any reason for wanting to see it?

RICHARDS: No. But I could have given them one. She's obviously very curious about you, Frazer. (*He drinks; looks at FRAZER*) Did you invite her here tonight?

FRAZER: Yes.

RICHARDS: Why?

FRAZER: She said she wanted to talk to me.

RICHARDS: (*Nodding*) Yes, well there you are.

FRAZER: You think she wants to talk about the film?

RICHARDS: I'm sure she does. You know that film is going to take a devil of a lot of explaining away.

FRAZER: I told her I wanted to include her in my memories of Amsterdam. She appeared satisfied.

RICHARDS looks dubious.

RICHARDS: That was before she saw the film. You overdid it, old boy.

FRAZER: You've seen it, then?

RICHARDS: Yes. (*Putting down his drink on the table*) I'd say you were including Amsterdam in your memories of Barbara Day!

FRAZER looks worried.

RICHARDS is enjoying FRAZER's uneasiness. Suddenly he appears to hear something outside and goes to the window and looks out.

RICHARDS: Here's your friend now!

FRAZER crosses over to the window.

CUT TO: The Mews seen through the window. Evening.
BARBARA DAY is getting out of her car. She crosses towards the entrance to FRAZER's flat.

CUT TO: FRAZER's Drawing Room. Evening.

RICHARDS and FRAZER are standing by the window, looking down into the mews.

RICHARDS: You'd better start thinking – fast. (*Indicating*) Is that the bedroom?

FRAZER: Yes.

RICHARDS: I'll wait in there. (*He indicated the drinks table*) May I?

FRAZER: Help yourself.

RICHARDS: Thanks.

RICHARDS crosses to the table and replenishes his drink. FRAZER watches him and then turns towards the hall. The front door bell is ringing.

RICHARDS turns from the table and crosses towards the bedroom.

RICHARDS: Make it convincing – and watch your step.

FRAZER looks at RICHARDS and goes into the hall.

A pause.

We hear the front door opening and the sound of voices.

RICHARDS quickly disappears into the bedroom.

BARBARA enters the drawing room, followed by FRAZER.

BARBARA: … I nearly telephoned you to say I couldn't make it …

FRAZER: I'm glad you didn't. But do you really have to go back to Hastings tonight?

BARBARA: Yes, I'm afraid so. Vivien's still there, arguing like mad with the auctioneer.

FRAZER: What happened?

BARBARA: Well, we bought this tallboy – or rather we thought we'd bought it – and then it transpired that another dealer, someone from Chester, had already made an offer for it and the offer had been accepted. At least, that's their story. Personally, I couldn't care less. They can keep

65

the tallboy. But that doesn't suit Vivien! Oh, dear, no! (*Faintly amused*) When I left you could hear her all over Hastings. "Fair's fair! No bloody nonsense, fair's fair!"

FRAZER: (*Laughing*) Well, let me get you a drink. What would you like?

BARBARA: I think I'd like a gin and tonic if you've got one.

FRAZER: Yes, of course. Do sit down.

BARBARA: Thank you. (*She sits; with a sigh*) I've had quite a day, what with one thing and another. Incidentally, has Arthur phoned you, by any chance?

FRAZER: (*At the drinks table; his back to BARBARA*) Arthur? Oh – your fiancé! No. No, he hasn't. Why do you ask?

BARBARA: I don't know. He started asking me about you the other night and I just wondered if he'd – been in touch with you? I think I told you, he hasn't been very well just lately, and when he's not well he invariably gets, well – jealous. That's the only word I can think of.

A slight pause.

FRAZER hands BARBARA the drink.

FRAZER: I hope that's all right.

BARBARA: Thank you.

A pause.

BARBARA sips her drink, smiling at FRAZER.

FRAZER: I think you said you saw the Inspector again, this morning?

BARBARA: Yes, I spent the best part of an hour with him.

FRAZER: That couldn't have been much fun.

BARBARA: Actually, it wasn't too bad because ... I asked to see him.

66

FRAZER: Really? Why did you do that?

A pause.

BARBARA: Tim, I've seen the film. Your film. The one they found on Cordwell.

FRAZER: (*Smiling; apparently quite pleased*) Have you? That's interesting. What was it like?

BARBARA: (*Laughing at FRAZER; almost searchingly*) Most of it was very good. Some of the shots of me were quite flattering, in fact, at least I thought so. (*After a moment, quietly*) But there's something I don't understand. Why were you following me, Tim?

FRAZER: Following you?

BARBARA: Yes. I was on that film far more than the Inspector realised. He only recognised me when I was in the foreground. But altogether you'd photographed me in six or seven different places. Now you're not going to tell me that it was coincidence that we both happened to be in those same places at the same time?

FRAZER: No, it wasn't coincidence. I was following you.

BARBARA appears disturbed by this statement.

BARBARA: Why?

FRAZER: I should have thought the reason was pretty obvious. (*He looks at BARBARA*)

BARBARA: But why follow me? You could have asked me to go out with you.

FRAZER: I did.

BARBARA: Yes, but that was after you'd taken the film, towards the end of my trip.

FRAZER: Yes, I know. I didn't approach you earlier because, well – I didn't want to spoil your holiday. I knew you wanted to be alone; to look

67

	at museums and art galleries ... Besides, you'd already mentioned the fact that you were engaged to someone ...
BARBARA:	(*Apparently relieved*) I see.
FRAZER:	You sound relieved.
BARBARA:	Yes, I am.
FRAZER:	But why did <u>you</u> think I'd been following you?
BARBARA:	(*After a slight hesitation*) I thought perhaps you were a detective or a private investigator of some sort.
FRAZER:	Why on earth should you think that?
BARBARA:	I don't know why, it's just that ... well, strange things have been happening to me just lately.
FRAZER:	What sort of things?

A pause.

BARBARA:	I think perhaps I'd better start at the beginning. About six weeks ago, when I was in Amsterdam, I ... (*She hesitates*)
FRAZER:	Go on, Barbara.
BARBARA:	I killed a man.
FRAZER:	Killed a man?
BARBARA:	Yes – in a car accident. His name was Leo Salinger. Oh, it was his own fault, they proved that at the inquest, but naturally I felt pretty badly about it. I wanted to do something to help him – his family, I mean. I tried to contact them but failed. I even consulted a lawyer friend of mine but he came up against exactly the same sort of thing that I did, just a blank wall.
FRAZER:	I see.
BARBARA:	And then when Cordwell was found murdered, in my flat, I began to wonder whether there was ... I know it sounds crazy, but I began to

wonder whether there was a connection between what happened to Cordwell and my car accident.

FRAZER: I don't see how there could have been, do you?

BARBARA: Not unless Cordwell knew Leo Salinger and he was trying to find out whether ...

FRAZER: Whether what?

BARBARA: (*Worried; agitated*) I don't know, Tim. I just don't know ...

FRAZER: If you ask me, I think this Cordwell business coming on top of the car accident has been too much for you.

BARBARA: Yes. Yes, you're probably right. (*She drinks*)

FRAZER: Finish your drink and let me get you another one.

BARBARA: Thank you, Tim. But I mustn't have another one. I'm driving out to Hastings. (*She looks at her watch and rises*)

FRAZER: Barbara, you've been asking me questions. Now, before you go, may I ask you one?

BARBARA: Yes, of course.

FRAZER: I've never really understood why you invited me to your flat that night – the night Cordwell was murdered. If your fiancé really is the jealous type ...

BARBARA: But I thought I'd explained that? I'd talked to Arthur about you and he said he wanted to get to know you. If I hadn't asked you to the flat he'd have probably thought that we were having an affair and I didn't want the two of you to meet. In fact, knowing Arthur, that's exactly what he would have thought. (*She looks at her watch again*) Tim, I'm sorry. But I must go, I really must! Thanks for the drink, darling. And I'm sorry I've got to rush away like this.

FRAZER: I'm sorry too, Barbara. But we really mustn't keep dear Vivien waiting!

BARBARA smiles at him and goes into the hall. FRAZER follows her.

After a moment RICHARDS comes out of the bedroom, glass in hand. He looks towards the hall, then crosses to the drinks table: he pours himself another drink.

FRAZER enters from the hall. He takes out his cigarettes and lights one. RICHARDS looks at him, thoughtfully sipping his drink.

FRAZER: Well?

RICHARDS: Can I give you a piece of advice, Frazer?

FRAZER: You mean about mixing business and – other things?

RICHARDS: Something like that, yes.

FRAZER smiles, a little bit superior.

RICHARDS: But you can take care of yourself, of course.

FRAZER: I think so.

RICHARDS looks at FRAZER with a wry smile. He feels in his pocket for something.

RICHARDS: A lot of other people have said the same thing. Perhaps Leo Salinger said it. Who knows.

There is such an ominous warning note in RICHARDS' words that the smile leaves FRAZER's face.

RICHARDS goes to him, taking CORDWELL's bulb catalogue from his pocket. He presents it to FRAZER.

RICHARDS: Here's the catalogue you asked for.

CUT TO: Lennard Street. Day.

FRAZER's car drives up and stops. FRAZER gets out of the car and crosses the road.

The barrow boy (VAN DAKAR) stands beside his barrow.

FRAZER passes him on the way to the coffee bar.
VAN DAKAR suddenly sees him.

VAN DAKAR: Morning, Guv! Don't forget the tip I gave you! "Fantasy" in the two-thirty. You can't go wrong!

FRAZER grins and strolls towards the coffee bar.
As FRAZER nears the coffee bar the door of the café opens and INSPECTOR TRUEMAN emerges into the street. The two men meet on the sidewalk.

TRUEMAN: Good morning, Mr Frazer!

FRAZER: Hello, Inspector!

TRUEMAN: (*Indicating the coffee bar*) If you're meeting Miss Day she hasn't arrived yet.

TEMPLE: I'm not meeting Miss Day.

TRUEMAN: Oh – I thought perhaps you were, sir, with her shop being just round the corner. My mistake.

FRAZER: Not to worry, we all make mistakes, Inspector.

TRUEMAN: Indeed we do. Oh – before I forget, sir! I wonder if you can help me. (*He takes an envelope from his pocket and extracts a postcard size photograph from it*) This gentleman is on our list of possible suspects, sir – although I suppose I shouldn't use the word suspect at this stage. I wondered if, by any chance, you'd ever come across him, Mr Frazer?

TRUEMAN hands FRAZER the photograph.
A pause.

FRAZER: (*After looking at the photograph*) No, I'm sorry. I don't know who he is and I've never seen him before.

TRUEMAN: (*Pleasantly*) Not to worry. (*He takes the photograph from FRAZER and returns it to the envelope; putting the envelope in his pocket*) Sorry you can't help me.

FRAZER: But I have helped you, Inspector. You've now got my fingerprints.

TRUEMAN, taken aback at being caught out, looks at FRAZER for a moment, then with a little laugh and a friendly wave goes on his way.

CUT TO: Inside The Amstel Coffee Bar. Day.

VIVIEN GILMORE is seated at a table. She has finished her coffee and is looking across at JAN who is behind the bar. She has just had a session with the INSPECTOR and is still somewhat irritated.

JAN crosses to her table to make out the bill. JAN is a dumpy, middle-aged Dutchman.

JAN: That's a lovely tallboy you've got in the shop, Miss Gilmore.

VIVIEN: Oh, so you've seen it! I'm glad you like it. We had to fight the battle of Hastings all over again to get possession of it.

JAN: How much are you asking for it?

VIVIEN: We haven't priced it yet. We only picked it up last night.

VIVIEN looks towards the doorway, seeing FRAZER come in. FRAZER sees VIVIEN and crosses to her table.

FRAZER: (*Indicating the vacant chair*) May I?

VIVIEN: Why not?

FRAZER sits.

VIVIEN accepts her bill from JAN.

VIVIEN: Thank you, Jan.

FRAZER quietly notes the name "JAN" and glances at the little man.

VIVIEN sorts out her change and pays her bill.

JAN: (*Accepting the money*) Thank you, Miss Gilmore.

FRAZER: Will you have another coffee?

VIVIEN: Thank you, no. I'm just going.

FRAZER: One coffee, please.

JAN nods and goes back to the bar for the coffee.

CAROL is busy there, serving.

VIVIEN: Are you meeting Barbara?

FRAZER: No.

VIVIEN: I wondered – because she hasn't arrived yet. Still, it's not surprising. We didn't get back from Hastings until two o'clock.

FRAZER: Did you win?

VIVIEN: Win?

FRAZER: The tallboy?

VIVIEN: Oh, yes! Yes, we won all right. We brought it back with us. Now of course, we're wondering whether we shall be able to sell it or not.

FRAZER: I'm sure you will.

VIVIEN is about to leave the table, then hesitates.

VIVIEN: Mr Frazer, do you happen to know an Inspector Trueman, by any chance?

FRAZER: Yes, of course. He's investigating the Cordwell murder. As a matter of fact, I've just bumped into him.

VIVIEN: Yes, I thought perhaps you might have done. (*Indicating FRAZER's chair*) He's been sitting in that chair for the past ten minutes asking me the most ridiculous questions you've ever heard.

FRAZER: About Barbara?

VIVIEN: Not only about Barbara. About you. About me. About the shop. (*Shaking her head*) I've read

73

	about murder cases, police investigations, that sort of thing – but never, in my wildest dreams, did I imagine it was anything like this!
FRAZER:	He's very thorough.
VIVIEN:	Thorough! I'm glad you think so. Do you know, he even asked me if I knew whether Cordwell had any appointments with a man called … Derekson …
FRAZER:	Ericson, surely?
VIVIEN:	… Oh, was that it? Well – obviously I'd never heard of anyone called Ericson. I'd never even heard of Cordwell until the poor devil was found murdered. Frankly, I think the man's an idiot, I really do. The Inspector, I mean …
FRAZER:	You could be right. (*Pleasantly; looking at VIVIEN*) On the other hand, I think you would be very unwise to underrate him.
VIVIEN:	Underrate him? Why should I? I'm an antique dealer, Mr Frazer. Believe you me, we're not in the habit of underrating people. If we did, we'd very soon be out of business. (*She rises*) Now, if you'll excuse me.
FRAZER:	(*Rising*) Yes, of course.
VIVIEN:	Goodbye.
FRAZER:	Goodbye, Miss Gilmore.

VIVIEN goes.

FRAZER sits, looking after her.

She nods at JAN as she leaves the coffee bar.

FRAZER's attention immediately focuses on JAN, although he does not look at him. Instead, he takes the bulb catalogue from his pocket, puts it on the table, and starts to read it.

JAN comes to the table with FRAZER's coffee. He puts the coffee on the table. He reacts to seeing the bulb catalogue.

FRAZER pretends he has just become aware of JAN and looks up at him.

FRAZER: Oh – thank you.

JAN is staring at FRAZER with interest. He glances at the catalogue.

FRAZER: Are you interested in bulbs?

JAN: *(After a slight hesitation)* When did <u>you</u> arrive?

FRAZER: *(Calmly)* You haven't answered my question.

JAN looks at FRAZER for a moment in silence, then walks away. FRAZER looks after him.

JAN goes behind the bar, takes something from the shelf underneath it, and goes back to FRAZER's table.

He is carrying a catalogue. He puts it on the table in front of FRAZER, taking up FRAZER's own catalogue. FRAZER looks at the new catalogue, then up at JAN. JAN points to a sticker on the cover of the catalogue.

JAN: This is a new one. It's up to date.

FRAZER looks down at the new catalogue. The sticker on the cover reads: "GORDON DEMPSEY: London Agents: 43a Long Acre, EC4 01-836 2011."

CUT TO: GORDON DEMPSEY's Office. Long Acre. London. Day.

This is an untidy, unimportant looking office, the wallpaper peeling here and there. The posters have been on the walls some time. All the posters show the tulip fields of Holland. A calendar on the wall advertises fertilisers, on top of a steel filing cabinet near the desk are several bottles of drink and some glasses.

GORDON DEMPSEY is seated at his desk, writing busily and smoking the remains of a cigar. He is a big, fattish man in his early fifties. There is a plate of half-eaten sandwiches at his side. The telephone rings.

DEMPSEY lifts the receiver.

75

DEMPSEY: International Bulb Importers …

For the duration of the following conversation we cut back and forth between DEMPSEY and FRAZER who is at the telephone in his flat.

FRAZER: Can I speak to Mr Gordon Dempsey, please?

DEMPSEY: Speaking.

FRAZER: Oh – good morning. I'm interested in buying some bulbs and your firm was recommended by a friend of mine.

DEMPSEY: What's the name of this friend?

FRAZER: Ericson.

DEMPSEY hesitates for a brief moment, but his manner is still brisk and businesslike. There is no great reaction to the name "Ericson".

DEMPSEY: I see. What's your name?

FRAZER: Scott. Norman Scott. You don't know me.

There is a slight pause.

FRAZER waits anxiously.

DEMPSEY: Have you got our catalogue?

FRAZER: Of course. Otherwise I couldn't have phoned you.

DEMPSEY: (*After a moment*) All right. I'll see you tonight. About six o'clock. You've got the address?

FRAZER: Yes, I've got it.

DEMPSEY: And bring the catalogue.

DEMPSEY replaces his receiver.

In his flat, FRAZER slowly replaces his own receiver and looks at it thoughtfully.

CUT TO: Long Acre. Day.

Outside Number 43a, showing the entrance to a large dilapidated block of offices.

FRAZER enters the hall. He looks up at the notice board to find out which floor DEMPSEY's office is on. He nods to himself and moves to the stairs.

CUT TO: Long Acre. Day.

FRAZER reaches the top of the stairs but doesn't know whether to go left or right. He looks at an office door number, then continues on down the corridor, looking at the numbers on the doors.

He stops at an office door, looking at it.

On the door a notice reads – "International Bulb Company – Regd. Offices – London and Hilversum".

FRAZER hesitates, then knocks on the door.

CUT TO: GORDON DEMPSEY's Office. Day.

DEMPSEY is at his desk, eating a sandwich. He puts the sandwich down and looks in the direction of the door on hearing FRAZER's knock.

DEMPSEY: Come in!

FRAZER enters.

FRAZER: Good evening …

DEMPSEY: (*Rising*) Mr Scott?

FRAZER: That's right.

DEMPSEY sits down again and indicates a chair.

FRAZER sits.

DEMPSEY studies him for a moment.

FRAZER's manner is casual, unhurried – but it conceals apprehension; he is not at all sure what to expect.

DEMPSEY: You've got the catalogue?

FRAZER: Yes.

FRAZER takes the catalogue from his pocket and hands it to DEMPSEY.

He looks at it, then hands it back to FRAZER.

DEMPSEY: Well, now … (*He picks up a pencil*) What would you like to order? Which ones do you want?

FRAZER looks at DEMPSEY, suddenly realising that this is the key question. After a moment he opens the catalogue and looks down at it.

FRAZER: I – er – haven't quite made up my mind …

DEMPSEY: I see. Well – we've got Piccadilly, Red Parrot, Fantasy, Octavius, Hilversum Red …

FRAZER looks up at the word "Fantasy".

FRAZER: (*After a momentary pause*) I'd like some Fantasy.

DEMPSEY nods.

DEMPSEY: How many?

FRAZER is thinking rapidly now. He decides to take a chance.

FRAZER: Oh – I should say – two-thirty …

DEMPSEY relaxes. He smiles for the first time.

DEMPSEY: All right, Mr Scott.

DEMPSEY takes a key from his pocket, unlocks the desk drawer and opens it.

FRAZER watches, filled with curiosity.

DEMPSEY takes an object from the drawer and places it on the desk in front of FRAZER. It is a metronome.

FRAZER stares at the metronome as DEMPSEY slowly leans forward and starts it.

END OF EPISODE THREE

EPISODE FOUR

OPEN TO: A Push-Button Telephone
A woman's gloved hand comes into view and slowly presses the numbers – 835 2011.

CUT TO: GORDON DEMPSEY's Office.
FRAZER is sitting staring at the metronome.
DEMPSEY is behind his desk, smiling. He is obviously waiting for FRAZER to react in a certain way, to say something perhaps.
FRAZER attempts to smile.
DEMPSEY's smile lessens somewhat; he looks a little curious.
DEMPSEY: Well, Mr Scott …?
The telephone rings.
DEMPSEY turns and lifts the receiver.
FRAZER looks a shade relieved.
DEMPSEY: (*Into the receiver*) International Bulb Importers
     …
A WOMAN's VOICE is heard at the other end.
FRAZER attempts to listen to this conversation without appearing to do so – DEMPSEY's eyes are on him all the time. He is still curious about FRAZER.
We can hear the WOMAN's VOICE, on the phone, tense and urgent, talking to DEMPSEY – but we cannot hear what she is saying or quite recognise the voice. It sounds like VIVIEN GILMORE.
DEMPSEY sits listening to her: his eyes on FRAZER.
FRAZER is convinced the telephone conversation concerns him – that someone is "tipping DEMPSEY off" about him. He tries desperately to look unconcerned but realises that his chances of bluffing his way out of the situation are now practically nil. He is accordingly urgently trying to figure out his next move.

DEMPSEY: (*After a long pause*) Yes, I've got it ... I get the picture. (*Impatiently*) Yes, I've told you – I understand perfectly.

DEMPSEY replaces the receiver; he has heard enough and realises that FRAZER has also heard enough.

DEMPSEY and FRAZER look at one another across the desk for a brief moment.

DEMPSEY stops the metronome.

FRAZER makes to rise from his chair.

DEMPSEY: But you're not going yet, surely? We haven't finished, Mr Scott – or should I say, Mr Frazer?

At the words "Mr Frazer" DEMPSEY quickly opens the desk drawer and reaches for a gun.

FRAZER rushes to the desk to intercept the movement.

As DEMPSEY takes the gun from the drawer, FRAZER knocks it from his hand and deals DEMPSEY a vicious blow on the jaw.

DEMPSEY slumps over the desk, temporarily out of it.

FRAZER snatches up the metronome and dashes out of the office.

DEMPSEY lies there, slumped over the desk. After a moment, he stirs, sits up, and looks around dazedly.

He sees the open door and rises to his feet.

He looks at the desk and realises that the metronome has gone.

Suddenly, angry with himself for letting FRAZER get away, he sweeps the plate of sandwiches from the desk onto the floor.

He remains there, breathing heavily.

CUT TO: The Library at 29 Marsham Square. London. Day.

ROSS is seated behind his desk; FRAZER seated opposite him; and LEWIS RICHARDS standing nearby. There are three metronomes on the desk.

They have evidently been discussing the metronomes which are the focus point of their attention at the moment.

ROSS: (*Indicating a metronome*) … And there's nothing at all out of the ordinary about this one – the one you got from Dempsey's office last night.

FRAZER: … In fact they're just three perfectly ordinary metronomes?

ROSS: Yes.

RICHARDS: Did this Dempsey character say anything when he produced it?

FRAZER: Nothing at all. He was obviously waiting for me to say something. He just put it on the desk and sat there, smiling. I was damn relieved when the phone rang.

ROSS smiles understandingly.

RICHARDS: And you think the voice at the other end was Vivien Gilmore's?

FRAZER: Yes, I think so – but I'm not really sure.

ROSS: Could it have been Barbara Day?

FRAZER: No. No, I'm pretty sure it wasn't Miss Day.

ROSS considers for a moment.

ROSS: Well – they're evidently on to you all right; but from what you've said they don't know who you are or what your game is.

FRAZER: No, but they'll only be too anxious to find out, which isn't going to make things any easier for me. They'll be watching me like a hawk.

RICHARDS: (*Musing*) That mightn't be such a bad thing.

ROSS looks at RICHARDS; gets his train of thought, and nods in agreement.

FRAZER looks from one to the other, not quite catching on.

ROSS: (*Consulting a folder on his desk*) Incidentally, we've now got some more information on

83

Cordwell. Apart from the odd spot of blackmail, it would appear our American friend also worked for Ericson: acting as a courier, bringing the stolen diamonds over to London. In fact, in my opinion, that's why he was murdered. Someone found out about this, killed him, and relieved him of the diamonds.

RICHARDS: You could be right. But what makes you think the murderer stole the diamonds?

ROSS: They weren't found on him.

RICHARDS: That's true, but surely there's a very simple explanation.

ROSS: Well – what is it? I'm all for simple explanations, Richards, you know that.

RICHARDS: Cordwell could have delivered the diamonds to Ericson before he was murdered, before going to Barbara Day's flat.

ROSS: (*Thoughtfully*) Yes, you're right. He could have done.

FRAZER: (*Quietly, but with emphasis*) He could have done – but he didn't.

Both ROSS and RICHARDS look at FRAZER, taken by surprise.

ROSS: You sound pretty definite, Mr Frazer.

FRAZER: I am. When Cordwell entered Barbara Day's flat he had the diamonds with him.

RICHARDS: How do you know?

RICHARDS and ROSS are looking at FRAZER now, unable to disguise their curiosity.

FRAZER: Let me tell you what happened last night after I left Dempsey's office with the metronome. I had my car parked in Long Acre near Dempsey's office. I put the metronome in the boot, locked it, and then drove like a bat in hell

84

out of the area, just in case Dempsey had any ideas of following me. As soon as I had a chance to collect my thoughts, I realised the first thing I had to do was to go back to Lennard Street …

CUT TO: Inside FRAZER's car. Evening.
FRAZER is driving his car.
FRAZER: (*Voice over*) I wanted to see that barrow boy. Whoever he was he must have known that I was heading for a meeting with Gordon Dempsey because he'd tipped me off with the code words – Fantasy in the two-thirty. Looking back and trying to remember the barrow boy's face I had a shrewd idea that he might have been one of the men who raided my flat and left the note in my cigarettes – the note which first directed me to Lennard Street.

CUT TO: Lennard Street. Evening.
FRAZER's car drives up and stops. FRAZER gets out.
FRAZER: (*Voice over*) Though why the same man should tip me off twice like that and also raid my flat, I couldn't imagine.
FRAZER looks up and down the street. His face lights up as he sees the barrow in the distance.
The BARROW BOY has his back to the camera, serving a customer.
FRAZER walks towards the barrow.
FRAZER: (*Voice over*) I stopped halfway down Lennard Street and spotted his barrow about a hundred yards down the street. I was in luck – or so I thought.
The customer walks away.

FRAZER goes up to the BARROW BOY who turns to FRAZER and we see that it is <u>not</u> VAN DAKAR, just an ordinary barrow boy. FRAZER's face drops.

BARROW BOY: Yes, Guv?

FRAZER: Oh – er – a pound of apples, please.

BARROW BOY: Right, Guv!

The BARROW BOY proceeds to weigh the apples and puts them in a bag.

FRAZER: Where's your mate? The chap that was here this morning?

BARROW BOY: Oh – 'im. (*Cagily*) 'E's not 'ere tonight.

FRAZER: I can see that.

The BARROW BOY holds out the bag of apples.

FRAZER takes out a ten-pound note.

FRAZER: Can you change ten pounds?

BARROW BOY: Ain't you got anything smaller?

FRAZER continues to hold the note and carries on talking.

FRAZER: Tell me something about your mate and you needn't bother with the change.

The BARROW BOY looks at the ten-pound note, then looks suspiciously at FRAZER.

FRAZER: (*Continuing his narration*) Once I'd assured him that I wasn't a policeman he told me everything he knew – which wasn't much. His own name was George Williams. He'd met the man I was looking for in a pub one night. The man had told George that he was an author looking for local colour. He said he was writing a book on the fruit trade and Covent Garden market in the old days. He offered George twenty-five quid a day for the use of his barrow. I asked George if he'd be seeing him again and he said "Yes", he thought he might be. I then told him it was important, very important, that his friend contact me and I gave him my card with my telephone number on it.

FRAZER gives the BARROW BOY his card, then hands him the note, at the same time dismissing the offer of the apples.
The BARROW BOY thanks him.
FRAZER goes.
The BARROW BOY pockets the ten-pound note as he looks after FRAZER, a little perplexed by it all.

CUT TO:　　　　　Lennard Street. Evening.
FRAZER's parked car.
FRAZER walks up to the car and is just about to open the door of the car when he notices someone a little further along the street.

FRAZER:　　　　(*Voice over*) I left Williams and was just getting into my car when I noticed Arthur Fairlee on the corner.

ARTHUR FAIRLEE is trying to hail a taxi. He makes to run for one, then sees someone has got there before him. He makes a gesture of irritation.

FRAZER:　　　　(*Voice over*) He was trying to get a taxi. As it was the tail-end of the rush hour he wasn't having much success.

FRAZER greets ARTHUR FAIRLEE and indicates his car, offering him a lift.

FRAZER:　　　　(*Voice over*) I offered him a lift and he accepted gratefully. He had a business appointment in Knightsbridge and was already fifteen minutes late.

FRAZER and FAIRLEE return to FRAZER's car.
FRAZER opens the door for FAIRLEE who gets in.
FRAZER gets into the driver's seat and the car drives off.

FRAZER: (*Voice over*) I'd only met Fairlee once before and on that occasion I couldn't quite weigh him up. I thought it might be useful to have another chat with him.

CUT TO: Inside FRAZER's car. Evening.

FRAZER and ARTHUR FAIRLEE are seated side by side, FRAZER driving. They have stopped temporarily in a traffic jam.

FRAZER: The traffic's always pretty heavy at this time.

ARTHUR FAIRLEE looks at his watch.

FRAZER: I'll turn off on the right here when we get moving. It's a bit longer but it'll probably be quicker.

FAIRLEE: Yes. (*A moment*) You know, this is frightfully kind of you. I do appreciate it.

FRAZER: Not at all. I know what it is when you're looking for a taxi. They never seem to turn up when you want one …

A slight pause.

FAIRLEE: Frazer, forgive me asking, but has that Inspector fellow been bothering you lately?

FRAZER: Trueman? No – I've seen him. In fact I bumped into him only this morning, but I wouldn't say he'd been troubling me, exactly.

FAIRLEE: You bumped into him, you say? Now that's interesting.

FRAZER looks at FAIRLEE.

FAIRLEE: If you ask me the blighter makes a habit of bumping into people. Only this lunchtime he bumped into yours truly just as I was leaving my club. And you'll never guess, not in a thousand years, what he talked about. Or rather, I should say, <u>who</u> he talked about.

88

FRAZER: Who he talked about? Your fiancée?

FAIRLEE: No.

FRAZER: Miss Gilmore?

FAIRLEE: No. Guess again.

FRAZER: Well – er …

FAIRLEE: You, Mr Frazer.

FRAZER: Me?

FAIRLEE: Yes. He wanted to know if I was a friend of yours. And in spite of the fact that I said I wasn't – that I'd only met you once – he still persisted in asking me questions about you.

FRAZER: What sort of questions?

FAIRLEE: He wanted to know what you were doing in Holland. Why you went there.

FRAZER: And what did you say?

FAIRLEE: What could I say? I said I hadn't the slightest idea what you were doing there. (*A moment*) Incidentally, it's none of my business, but what were you doing in Amsterdam? Were you on holiday?

FRAZER: Not exactly. I'm an engineer by profession and unfortunately my company went broke.

FAIRLEE: Yes, I know. Barbara told me.

FRAZER: Years ago I used to write for a trade magazine and the editor, an old friend of mine, asked me if I'd like to write one or two articles on Holland with particular emphasis on their export problems. I don't know why he asked me. I think he thought I was up against it. Anyway, I enjoyed writing the articles and quite apart from a very good fee the magazine also paid my expenses. So I didn't do too badly.

FAIRLEE: It doesn't sound like it.

A slight pause.

FRAZER:	Did the Inspector ask you anything else?
FAIRLEE:	Yes, he asked me if I'd heard of anyone called Ericson. I said I hadn't. I gather he asked Vivien the same question.
FRAZER:	Yes.
FAIRLEE:	Who is Ericson, do you know?
FRAZER:	He was a friend of Cordwell's. According to the Inspector that's why Cordwell came here, to meet Ericson.
FAIRLEE:	Did he meet him?
FRAZER:	I don't know. You'd better ask the Inspector that question the next time he bumps into you.
FAIRLEE:	I haven't the slightest intention of asking him anything. In fact, if I have my way I'll never set eyes on the chap again.
FRAZER:	I know how you feel. He's what I call "the ultra- persistent type".
FAIRLEE:	(*Amused*) My dear fellow, how right you are! The ultra-persistent type! I'll have to remember that and trot it out at our next board meeting …

CUT TO: Knightsbridge. Night.
FRAZER's car drives up and stops. ARTHUR FAIRLEE gets out of the car, waves to FRAZER, and hurries into a nearby block of offices.
The car drives off.

CUT TO: The Library at 29 Marsham Square. Day.
ROSS is seated at his desk, RICHARDS is standing nearby; they are listening to FRASER as he tells his story. We hear FRAZER's voice but do not see him.

| FRAZER: | (*Out of vision*) … After I'd dropped Arthur Fairlee in Knightsbridge, I went back to my flat. About a quarter of an hour later I had a |

phone call from Barbara Day. She was on her way to Windsor and she asked if she could drop in and see me. She arrived at about half-past seven and was obviously very worried about something. She said she couldn't stay long as she was picking up Vivien Gilmore in half an hour. Apparently she'd been at the shop all day but had slipped back to her flat to change her dress before meeting her partner.

CUT TO: FRAZER's Drawing Room. Evening.
BARBARA DAY is seated in an armchair, talking to FRAZER.
She has an empty glass in her hand.

BARBARA: When I arrived home everything seemed perfectly normal; the flat was just as I'd left it this morning. At least, I thought it was – until I went to the wardrobe.

FRAZER: The wardrobe?

BARBARA: Yes. You see – this dress – (*She indicates the one she is wearing*) I don't wear it very often but I thought I'd wear it tonight. I went to the wardrobe and it – well, it wasn't where I'd left it.

FRAZER: You mean someone's been in your flat?

BARBARA: (*Nodding*) Yes. I'm sure someone's been there since I left this morning.

FRAZER: You couldn't have moved the dress yourself and forgotten about it?

BARBARA: I might have, I suppose. But I found other things had been moved. Things I mightn't have noticed in the ordinary way. I'm positive someone's been through the flat, Tim, looking for something.

FRAZER: Looking for what, exactly?

91

BARBARA: That's just it! I don't know. There was some money in one of the drawers, and a box of jewellery – nothing madly expensive, but certainly not worth ignoring.

FRAZER: And there's nothing missing?

BARBARA: No; nothing at all – so far as I know.

FRAZER: Have you told anyone else about this?

BARBARA: No, I haven't. I was going to ring Inspector Trueman, but then I thought – why bother? Ten to one he won't believe me anyway.

FRAZER: Why do you say that?

B ARBARA: Maybe it's just my imagination but I think – well, let's face it, Tim. Right now I'm his favourite suspect.

FRAZER: Nonsense, Barbara! If he really thought you'd murdered Cordwell …

BARBARA: Oh, I don't say he'd go as far as that. But I'm sure he thinks I was friendly with Cordwell; probably having an affair with him. Incidentally, I don't know whether you know it or not, but apparently Cordwell was a pretty disreputable character.

FRAZER: Who told you that?

BARBARA: The Inspector did.

FRAZER: The Inspector?

BARBARA: Yes. He was watching me like a hawk at the time; I think he wanted to see what my reaction was.

FRAZER: Did he tell you anything else about Cordwell?

BARBARA: Only that he'd been staying at a hotel on the Cromwell Road. When they searched his room they found a suitcase full of clothes and a box of cigars – nothing else.

FRAZER: (*Nodding*) Come to think of it, you never saw him without a cigar in his mouth, even when he wasn't actually smoking …

BARBARA: Trueman wanted to know if I could identify any of the clothes. He showed me several of Cordwell's things. Including that terrible sports jacket he wore in Amsterdam.

FRAZER: (*His thoughts elsewhere*) Sports jacket? Oh, yes – yes, I remember.

BARBARA: You couldn't fail to remember it! (*Putting the glass down; rising*) Anyway, Tim, I feel much better now we've had this talk. It was just that – well, someone coming into your house and going through your things – it's a horrible feeling.

FRAZER: Yes, I know. But I shouldn't worry too much about it.

BARBARA: You don't think that whoever it was, will … come back?

FRAZER: No, I don't. From what you say they obviously searched the place pretty thoroughly, which means they either found what they were looking for or they didn't. In either case, they're not likely to come back.

BARBARA: Well – I hope you're right. And thank you again, darling, for listening to me, although I really shouldn't have bothered you with all this. I should have talked to Arthur.

FRAZER: (*Looking at BARBARA; quietly*) Why didn't you?

A moment, then:

BARBARA: To be honest, I didn't think of it. I thought of you.

BARBARA smiles, their eyes hold, then she moves to the door, followed by FRAZER.

CUT TO: The Mews outside FRAZER's Flat. Evening.
BARBARA's car is parked outside FRAZER's flat.
FRAZER and BARBARA come out of the flat and walk to the car, talking together.
FRAZER: (*Continuing his narration*) I saw Barbara Day down to her car and just as she was leaving she said she'd invited Vivien to dinner the following night and would I care to join them? Naturally – I said I would.

BARBARA smiles at FRAZER as he helps her into her car. She gives a friendly wave and drives off.
FRAZER: After she'd gone I thought over something I'd had at the back of my mind ever since she'd talked about Cordwell.

FRAZER stands looking thoughtfully after the car.
He takes out a cigarette and lights it.
FRAZER: It was the box of cigars the police had found in Cordwell's room. The little I saw of Cordwell he was never without a cigar in his mouth. He smoked them in a cigar holder. And yet when they found his body, curiously enough, there was no cigar, or cigar holder, near it. At that moment an idea occurred to me. It was only a shot in the dark, but I knew Barbara was going to be away from her flat for at least a couple of hours, so I thought the idea I had was well worth pursuing.

During the above narration, FRAZER throws away his cigarette in a moment of sudden decision, goes into his garage, gets into his car and starts the engine.

94

FRAZER's car drives out of the garage and off down the Mews.

CUT TO: BARBARA DAY's Flat. Evening.
The front door of the flat.
FRAZER stands at the door. He looks up and down the corridor, then quickly takes a bunch of keys from his pocket. He tries several keys, before finally succeeding in opening the door.

FRAZER: I arrived at about a quarter past eight and after a little difficulty, and using one of the gadgets you provided me with, I let myself into the flat.

CUT TO: BARBARA DAY's Flat. The Hall.
FRAZER comes in and closes the door.
He stands there for a moment in a listening attitude.
Once assured that all is quiet, he moves into the living room.
He stands in the doorway and surveys the room.

CUT TO: BARBARA DAY's Flat. The Living Room.
FRAZER: (*Voice over*) I knew what I was looking for – and I knew that someone else had already done a thorough job of searching the room – so the obvious places were out. I remember the spot where I'd found Cordwell and I decided to try and put myself in his shoes, when faced by whoever it was that killed him.

FRAZER is standing in the doorway looking at the spot on the floor. Deliberately, he takes a cigarette from a packet of cigarettes and puts it in his mouth. He returns the cigarette packet to his pocket and stands there thoughtfully for a moment.

Slowly, he walks towards the "murder spot". He stops suddenly about a yard or so from the spot as though confronted by an attacker.

In an obvious manner he takes the cigarette from his mouth and slings it aside, keeping his eyes riveted on his "attacker".

He looks to see where the cigarette has fallen and goes to it, bending down.

It is on the floor near the waste basket. This is near the electric fire but this much is not apparent at the moment.

He takes up the cigarette and puts it in his breast pocket, his attention immediately focussing on the waste basket. He empties it, finding only some torn notepaper. He returns the paper to the basket and looks around him.

He sees the electric fire in the fireplace. He goes quickly to it, sees it is removable and takes the electric fire from the grate.

He looks into the grate and finds what he is looking for. He reaches excitedly into the grate and takes out a half-burnt cigar in a holder. He looks at it with a satisfied smile, then crosses quickly to the table.

He takes a penknife from his pocket, also a handkerchief. He spreads the handkerchief on the table, places the cigar on it and cuts it open.

He continues to shred the cigar but finds nothing. His attention turns to the cigar holder.

He fiddles with it for a moment. His eyes suddenly light up as he finds the end unscrews.

He unscrews the end of the holder and two diamonds fall out into the palm of his hand.

CUT TO: The Library at 29 Marsham Square.

The diamonds are in ROSS's hand. He, FRAZER and RICHARDS are looking down at the diamonds.

FRAZER: I expected to find them in the cigar – if I found them at all, that is. It never occurred to me that they'd be in the holder.

ROSS: Getting as far as the cigar was good thinking. Frazer.

ROSS picks up the cigar holder which is lying on the desk. RICHARDS holds out his hand for the diamonds.

RICHARDS: (*To ROSS*) May I, sir?

ROSS hands RICHARDS the diamonds. RICHARD inspects them closely. Meanwhile, ROSS examines the cigar holder, unscrewing it.

RICHARDS: (*After a moment*) Well, I'd say this little lot's worth somewhere between seventy and eighty thousand, on present day prices.

FRAZER looks at RICHARDS, obviously surprised. ROSS smiles at FRAZER's reaction.

ROSS: You can take his word for it, Frazer. He used to be in the diamond business.

RICHARDS: (*Nodding; handing the diamonds back to ROSS*) I packed it in – there was no money in it.

FRAZER: Between seventy and eighty thousand, you say?

RICHARDS: Yes, and I'm not far out, Frazer, I assure you. (*Looking at the cigar holder*) You know, whoever it was murdered Cordwell couldn't have considered the cigar holder as a possible hiding place.

FRAZER: No. He just thought it natural for Cordwell to dispense with the cigar before the fight started. It didn't occur to him to look for it after he'd killed Cordwell.

ROSS: We're assuming, of course, that the murderer was after the diamonds …

RICHARDS: I don't see what else he could have been after. Don't forget all those things in the zipper bag had been turned out and searched through.

FRAZER: Yes, it must have been the diamonds.

RICHARDS: Well, one thing we do know – for sure. Cordwell hadn't kept his appointment with Ericson.

ROSS: No, but he must have been on the point of doing so.

FRAZER: You mean –?

ROSS: I mean he'd obviously arranged to meet Ericson at Barbara Day's flat – otherwise, what the devil was he doing there?

FRAZER shakes his head, obviously defeated.

RICHARDS: Frazer, about this phoney barrow boy. The one who gave you the tip about the bulb catalogue. You think he might have been one of the men who raided your flat?

FRAZER: It's possible, but I couldn't be sure. I only caught a glimpse of his face just before he hit me.

ROSS: What was the other man like – the one you spoke to?

FRAZER: (*Thinking*) Dark; thickset – fairly well dressed …

RICHARDS: (*To ROSS*) He's probably one of Ericson's people.

FRAZER: Then who's the other man – the barrow boy – is he one of them, too?

ROSS: (*Nodding*) Yes, I think so. And for some reason or other he's double-crossing him. (*He looks at FRAZER*) If you saw him again, do you think you'd recognise him?

FRAZER thinks about this.

FRAZER: It depends. Dressed as a barrow boy, yes, I
                   would. But in different clothes – I'm not
                   sure.

CUT TO: Lennard Street. Evening.
VAN DAKAR is talking to GEORGE WILLIAMS, the genuine
barrow boy, near the barrow.
VAN DAKAR is wearing a lounge suit now – the one he was
wearing when we saw him searching FRAZER's flat. He is
looking down at the card given to him by GEORGE
WILLIAMS – FRAZER's card.
WILLIAMS: …Give me a tenner, too.
VAN DAKAR: When was this?
WILLIAMS: Last night. I'd say about – let's see – quarter
                   past six, summat like that. That's all he said
                   – just to give you that.
VAN DAKAR: Thank you, George. I appreciate your help.
VAN DAKAR gives WILLIAMS a friendly nod and hurries
away, glancing down at the card as he goes.
He goes into a telephone box, takes some coins from his
pocket, lifts the receiver, and looking at the card in his hand,
dials a number.

CUT TO: FRAZER's Drawing Room. Evening.
FRAZER comes out of the bedroom, carrying his hat and
coat, and crosses towards the hall.
The telephone rings.
FRAZER goes to the phone and picks up the receiver.
FRAZER: (*On the phone*) Hello?
We intercut between FRAZER in his drawing room and VAN
DAKAR in the telephone box for the following dialogue.
VAN DAKAR hears the "pay tone" and puts coins into the
box.
VAN DAKAR: Is that Mr Frazer?

FRAZER: Yes, speaking.

VAN DAKAR: My name is Van Dakar …

FRAZER: Van –

VAN DAKAR: Van Dakar.

FRAZER looks bewildered.

VAN DAKAR: I understand you'd like to see me, Mr Frazer. George Williams, the barrow boy, gave me your card. He said you wanted me to phone you …

FRAZER: That's quite right. I thought it might be a very good idea if you and I got together, Mr Van Dakar.

VAN DAKAR: (*With the suggestion of a smile*) Yes. Yes, indeed. It might be a very good idea, Mr Frazer.

FRAZER: Then perhaps we could arrange to meet sometime?

VAN DAKAR: Yes, certainly. Tonight?

FRAZER: Tonight? Yes – that's fine. (*Suddenly remembering*) But I'm afraid it will have to be late. I've got a dinner date.

VAN DAKAR: Well, let's say eleven-forty-five – would that suit you?

FRAZER: Yes, splendid. Where shall we meet?

VAN DAKAR: What's the number of your car?

FRAZER: My car? TGP 951R.

VAN DAKAR writes this down on the card GEORGE WILLIAMS gave him as he continues talking.

VAN DAKAR: Drive into Berkeley Square and wait opposite Bruton Street – near the car showroom.

FRAZER: I'll be there …

VAN DAKAR: Just wait in the car – I'll find you.

FRAZER: Yes, all right. Thanks for … (*About to ring off*)

VAN DAKAR: (*Stopping FRAZER*) Just a minute … Did you say you were dining with Miss Day this evening?

FRAZER is taken aback by VAN DAKAR's remark.

FRAZER: No, I didn't. But I am.

VAN DAKAR: (*Smiles to himself*) Well, in that case, I'd skip the coffee, Mr Frazer.

VAN DAKAR replaces the receiver, still smiling.

FRAZER looks at the receiver in his hand – puzzled by VAN DAKAR's words.

CUT TO: Lennard Street. Evening.

In the telephone box, VAN DAKAR takes up the card with FRAZER's car number on it and turns to go out of the box.

As he does so there is the loud roar of a passing car, followed by a series of shots. The noise of breaking glass is heard as the bullets hit the telephone box, followed by a sudden swell of excited voices.

VAN DAKAR clutches the coin meter; holding his side – he has been hit and is in obvious pain.

END OF EPISODE FOUR

EPISODE FIVE

OPEN TO: The Telephone Box. Lennard Street. Evening.
VAN DAKAR has been shot and his body is on the floor of the
telephone booth. There is a background of excited voices and
the sound of an approaching ambulance.

CUT TO: The Front door of FRAZER's Flat. Evening.
INSPECTOR TRUEMAN is standing at the door, his finger on
the bell. We hear the bell ringing inside the flat.

CUT TO: The Hall of FRAZER's Flat. Evening.
FRAZER comes out of the drawing room and opens the front
door. He is surprised to find himself facing the INSPECTOR.
FRAZER: Good evening, Inspector.
TRUEMAN: Good evening, sir. May I come in?
FRAZER: Yes, certainly.
TRUEMAN enters the hall.
FRAZER closes the front door.
FRAZER: (*Indicating the drawing room*) Please go in …

CUT TO: FRAZER's Drawing Room. Evening.
FRAZER follows TRUEMAN into the room, indicating a
chair. The INSPECTOR nods and sits.
FRAZER: Can I offer you a drink?
TRUEMAN: No, thank you, sir.
FRAZER: (*After a moment*) Well, Inspector?
TRUEMAN: We've come across certain information
concerning Mr Cordwell, sir, and since you're
obviously involved in this affair – to a certain
extent, at any rate – I thought perhaps you
might be interested to hear what we've
discovered.
FRAZER: I'm interested, Inspector.
TRUEMAN: Apparently Cordwell had quite a reputation in
America. In fact, he served a five-year

105

sentence over there for blackmail. (*He watches FRAZER as he speaks*) He was also a dealer, if that's the correct term, in stolen diamonds.

FRAZER: Stolen diamonds? Well, he certainly fooled me – on the one occasion I met him, that is. I thought he was just an ordinary tourist. He couldn't have been more typical.

TRUEMAN: Yes, well, there you are. (*A moment*) In view of what we now know about him the motive for murder would appear to be pretty obvious. Whoever murdered Cordwell was after the diamonds he was carrying.

FRAZER: But you don't know, for certain, that he was carrying diamonds on that particular occasion.

TRUEMAN: No, that's true, we don't. But in view of his record and reputation it seems a pretty safe assumption. Don't you agree, Mr Frazer?

FRAZER: No, I don't – not entirely. However, I'm sure that's not the only reason why you came to see me, to tell me about Cordwell.

TRUEMAN: You're quite right, it's not the only reason. (*After a slight pause*) As I understand it, from the statement you made, you didn't go near Miss Day's flat on the night of the murder?

FRAZER: That's correct. I didn't.

TRUEMAN: Miss Day invited you to the flat for drinks and to meet her fiancé, Mr Fairlie, but you didn't turn up.

FRAZER: (*Nodding*) I suddenly discovered I had an appointment.

TRUEMAN: A business appointment in Guildford?

FRAZER: That's quite right. But surely you've checked on that, Inspector?

TRUEMAN:	No, sir – not yet.
FRAZER:	I'm delighted to hear it. It shows you have a trusting nature after all.
TRUEMAN:	Thank you, sir. (*Smiling*) But I wouldn't depend on it, if I were you. Now, if you've no objections, I'd like to talk about the following morning.
FRAZER:	The following morning?
TRUEMAN:	Yes. The morning after the murder. I gather it was then that you paid your first visit to Miss Day.
FRAZER:	(*Puzzled*) Yes …
TRUEMAN:	And you'd never visited her before?
FRAZER:	No, I hadn't.
TRUEMAN:	You're quite sure about that?
FRAZER:	Of course I'm sure!
TRUEMAN:	(*Suddenly, with authority, making his point*) Then how can you account for the fact that your fingerprints were found on the inside door of Miss Day's flat? (*Before FRAZER can speak*) They were discovered on the night of the murder, Mr Frazer – before your visit the following morning.

FRAZER is apparently lost for an answer.

FRAZER:	<u>My</u> fingerprints?
TRUEMAN:	Yes.
FRAZER:	But – it's impossible! Are you sure they were my fingerprints?
TRUEMAN:	Quite sure. (*A moment; watching FRAZER*) It's not too late to have second thoughts, Mr Frazer, if by any chance, something slipped your mind?
FRAZER:	Nothing slipped my mind, Inspector!

TRUEMAN: What I mean, sir – if you wish to change your story in any way, the fact that you've already told me …

FRAZER: I haven't the slightest desire to change my story! And use your head, Inspector! Even if I had turned up – how the devil would I have got into the flat?

TRUEMAN: You could have used the fire escape, it's a perfectly good one. I know, because I tested it.

FRAZER: That's as maybe; but I didn't use it, Inspector.

TRUEMAN: Very well, Mr Frazer, if you say so. (*He rises*) And you can't account for your fingerprints?

FRAZER: No, I'm afraid I can't.

TRUEMAN: I see. Well, I'm sorry to have taken up so much of your time.

The INSPECTOR goes out into the hall, followed by FRAZER.

CUT TO: The Hall.

TRUEMAN is moving towards the front door as the door bell rings.
TRUEMAN hesitates, looking back at FRAZER.
FRAZER looks at TRUEMAN a little uneasily.

FRAZER: It seems to be one of those evenings …

FRAZER opens the front door.
RICHARDS is revealed in the doorway. He looks at FRAZER, then at the INSPECTOR.

FRAZER: Oh, hello! Come in!

RICHARDS enters; looking at TRUEMAN.

RICHARDS: Good evening.

TRUEMAN: Evening, sir.

FRAZER: Oh – Inspector Trueman – Mr Richards …

RICHARDS nods to the INSPECTOR.

RICHARDS: Turned chilly.

TRUEMAN: Yes. Yes, it has. Good night, sir. Good night, Mr Frazer.

FRAZER: Good night, Inspector.

TRUEMAN: (*Turning*) Oh, I shall probably want to talk to you again, fairly soon. You won't be going away or anything?

FRAZER: No. No, I shall be here for the next few weeks at least.

TRUEMAN: Thank you, sir. Good night.

FRAZER: Good night.

TRUEMAN goes.

FRAZER closes the door and looks ruefully at RICHARDS.

RICHARDS: Well? What's all that about?

FRAZER: I left my fingerprints on the inside door of Barbara Day's flat.

RICHARDS: (*With a faint smile*) You should watch things like that, Frazer.

FRAZER: (*Going into the drawing room*) Yes, well – I didn't know I was going to find Cordwell there.

CUT TO: The Drawing Room.

FRAZER enters, followed by RICHARDS.

FRAZER: I've had two surprises this evening – there's sure to be a third. What brings you here?

RICHARDS takes a photograph from his wallet and holds it out towards FRAZER.

RICHARDS: I'd like you to take a look at this photograph.

FRAZER takes the photograph and looks at it. It is a polaroid of VAN DAKAR's face. He is lying on a stretcher, his eyes closed.

FRAZER: That's him! That's the barrow boy – the one who gave me the tip! (*Looking at*

109

RICHARDS) And it is the man who knocked me out – I'm sure of that now!

FRAZER looks at the photograph again; then looks up at RICHARDS.

FRAZER: But where was this taken?

RICHARDS: On a stretcher, en route to the hospital. The poor devil was shot after making a phone call from Lennard Street.

FRAZER: (*Shocked*) Lennard Street?

RICHARDS: Yes.

FRAZER: Richards, that call was to me! I was to meet him tonight; he asked me to … (*He stops; looking at the photograph again*) How bad is he?

RICHARDS: Pretty bad, I'm afraid. He's unconscious at the moment. His name's Van Dakar. He's a Dutchman.

FRAZER: But what happened – the shooting, I mean?

RICHARDS: (*With a shrug*) It was done from a fast car; no one identified them. (*Taking the photograph from FRAZER*) But tell me about the phone call.

FRAZER: We made arrangements to meet tonight, after I'd had dinner with Barbara Day. (*He looks at RICHARDS; hesitates*) Incidentally …

RICHARDS: Yes?

FRAZER: He knew I was dining with Barbara Day – he advised me to skip the coffee.

RICHARDS is obviously intrigued by this.

RICHARDS: Did he? Did he, indeed? That's interesting. (*He looks at FRAZER*) Sounds like good advice to me, Frazer. If I were you, I'd take it.

CUT TO: The Living Room of BARBARA DAY's Flat.
Night.

BARBARA, FRAZER and VIVIEN GILMORE have finished
dinner and are seated in comfortable chairs, talking.

BARBARA: ...I still don't see what all this has to do with
             you, Tim?

FRAZER: Well, it's really quite simple. (*Indicating the*
             door) They found some fingerprints on the
             inside of that door. They've checked them
             with mine. I regret to say, they're identical.

VIVIEN: (*Astonished*) Your fingerprints?

FRAZER: Yes.

BARBARA and VIVIEN stare at FRAZER for a moment; then
BARBARA relaxes.

BARBARA: But you came here the next morning! You'd
             have left your fingerprints all over the place.

FRAZER: Yes, but apparently these were found the
             night before – the night the murder was
             committed.

VIVIEN: But how could your fingerprints possibly be
             on that door the night the murder took place –
             if you didn't come here until the following
             morning?

FRAZER shrugs, saying nothing.
There is a pause.

VIVIEN: (*Thoughtfully*) Barbara didn't you tell me
             that you were expecting Mr Frazer that night?

BARBARA: Yes. Yes, I was. But he couldn't come. He
             had a business appointment in ... (*She looks*
             at FRAZER)

FRAZER: Guildford.

BARBARA: Guildford, that's right.

VIVIEN: (*To BARBARA*) If I remember rightly you
             slipped out for a little while, to see Arthur ...

BARBARA: Yes, I did.

VIVIEN: What time was that?

BARBARA: I suppose I left here at about ten to six.

VIVIEN: And when was Mr Frazer due?

BARBARA: Oh – half-past seven or thereabouts.

VIVIEN: And what time was it when you got back from Arthur's?

BARBARA: (*Rather intrigued by VIVIEN's questioning*) It must have been about half-past seven, perhaps a little later.

VIVIEN: So in actual fact, Cordwell must have already …

FRAZER: (*Interrupting VIVIEN; with an uneasy little laugh*) Hey, just a minute! You've been seeing too much of the Inspector! You're beginning to sound like him!

VIVIEN attempts a smile.

FRAZER: It's true I was due here at seven-thirty. But even if I'd turned up, how the devil could I have got in? Barbara wasn't here! In any case, I'm sorry to disappoint you, but I was in Guildford. (*To BARBARA*) I telephoned you from there, remember?

BARBARA: Yes, of course you did! (*She rises*) I'll get some coffee.

VIVIEN: Not for me, darling. I shan't sleep a wink if I drink coffee at this time of night.

The telephone rings.

BARBARA turns, hesitates.

VIVIEN: Shall I take it?

BARBARA shakes her head and crosses to the phone.

BARBARA: (*To FRAZER*) Excuse me, Tim. (*On the phone*) Hello … Yes … Oh, hello, Arthur! (*She glances across at VIVIEN, a little*

112

wearily) Yes, I'm listening ... Have you taken some of the tablets? ... Well, try them – they may do some good ... But they have in the past ... (*With a sigh*) All right, I'll come round later. In the meantime, just try and relax ... Yes, of course I will ... I don't know, Arthur, but I'll come round as soon as I can ... What's that? ... Yes, Vivien ... I've told you I will, Arthur ... Yes, dear ... (*She replaces the receiver*)

VIVIEN: What's the matter? Has he had one of his attacks?

BARBARA: I suppose so. I've got to the stage now when I don't know whether they're serious or not. I get urgent calls from him and then when I rush over there he seems reasonably all right. On the other hand, sometimes he really is ill – very ill – it's quite dreadful to watch him. (*She sighs*) But I do honestly think he trades on it every now and then.

VIVIEN: Of course he does! He always has done!

VIVIEN takes a cigarette from a box on the table.

BARBARA: But I must admit he sounded pretty awful ... I wonder if I ought to ...

FRAZER: (*Rising*) Look, Barbara, we've had a lovely evening and I've got to make a move anyway. (*He looks at his watch*) So please, don't consider me. In fact, if you want my opinion, I think you ought to take a look at him. It'll put your mind at rest.

BARBARA: Well – yes, I think perhaps you're right. I'm sorry about the coffee.

FRAZER: We'll have it some other time. Now, can I give you a lift?

113

BARBARA: No, thank you, Tim. I've got my car and I haven't the slightest idea how long I'll be. If you'll excuse me, I'm going to change my dress.

BARBARA goes into the bedroom.

FRAZER sees VIVIEN looking at him, holding the unlit cigarette in her hand.

FRAZER: Oh, I'm sorry.

FRAZER takes out his light and flicks it.

VIVIEN: (*Accepting the light*) Thank you. (*After a moment she looks at FRAZER*) You can give me a lift if you like, Mr Frazer.

FRAZER: Yes – of course. Delighted.

VIVIEN: Thank you.

FRAZER replaces his cigarette lighter in his pocket.

CUT TO: A Street in the West End of London. Night.

FRAZER's car is travelling down the street.

CUT TO: Inside FRAZER's Car. Night.

VIVIEN and FRAZER are sitting side by side in the front of the car. FRAZER is driving.

VIVIEN: … I've never been very keen on him myself. Reminds me of an uncle of mine. Oh, he was ill all right, but it was the people around him who suffered the most. That's how it is with Barbara and Arthur Fairlee.

FRAZER: She must be fond of him, I suppose?

VIVIEN: (*Shaking her head*) I don't think she is. If you ask me, she just feels sorry for him. One of these days she'll tell him to go to the devil.

FRAZER: (*With a faint smile*) Do you really think so?

VIVIEN: I'm sure of it. Besides, a stockbroker's not really Barbara's type. (*She looks at FRAZER*) You're an engineer, aren't you?

FRAZER: I was. Had my own firm, but it went bust. Now I'm trying my hand at journalism.

VIVIEN: Bit of a drastic change, surely?

FRAZER: Yes. I've sold a few articles to trade papers, but that's about all. In fact, I'm pretty desperate at the moment.

VIVIEN: Really?

FRAZER: (*Nodding*) I'd try anything that would help to pay the rent. (*Suddenly; as if the thought had just occurred to him*) Oh dear, I shouldn't have said that. Please, don't mention this to Barbara ...

VIVIEN: No, of course not.

There is a pause.

VIVIEN looks thoughtful.

VIVIEN: I was just thinking about what the Inspector told you ...

FRAZER: About Cordwell?

VIVIEN: Yes – about him being in the diamond business. You know, I wouldn't be a bit surprised if the murderer didn't get quite a haul that night.

FRAZER: Well, if he did I doubt whether it'd do him much good.

VIVIEN: What do you mean?

FRAZER: I've always been given to understand that stolen goods – diamonds in particular – were difficult to get rid of.

VIVIEN: Well, obviously Cordwell knew how to get rid of them.

FRAZER: Yes, but he was in the business. He had a ready market. Probably through that chap Trueman mentioned.

VIVIEN: Ericson?

FRAZER: (*Nodding*) That's right. Cordwell had several appointments with him, remember.

A pause.

VIVIEN: Well, anyway, one good thing has come out of all this. It's made Barbara take another look at Arthur Fairlee, and at long last I think she's beginning to see the light. He's shown no concern for her at all throughout the whole of this business. On the other hand, you've been quite the opposite.

FRAZER looks at VIVIEN.

VIVIEN: Barbara said that herself.

FRAZER: Did she?

VIVIEN: Yes, she did.

FRAZER makes no comment; he looks ahead.

VIVIEN: (*After a moment; quietly*) Oh – drop me on the corner here, will you?

FRAZER: Yes, of course.

FRAZER switches on the indicator light.

CUT TO: A Street Corner. Night.

FRAZER's car draws up at the kerb.

VIVIEN gets out, thanks FRAZER for the lift, and goes off down the street.

FRAZER's car pulls away from the kerb.

CUT TO: The Front Door of FRAZER's Flat. Day.

LEWIS RICHARDS is ringing the door bell. He carries a small case.

After a moment, FRAZER opens the door. He is wearing a dressing gown.

FRAZER: Oh – good morning! Come in!

RICHARDS enters the flat.

116

CUT TO: The Hall.

FRAZER: You're bright and early.

RICHARDS smiles.

FRAZER closes the door and leads the way into the drawing room, after glancing down at the case RICHARDS is carrying.

CUT TO: The Drawing Room.

FRAZER enters, followed by RICHARDS.

RICHARDS: (*Pointedly*) Did you have a good night's sleep?

FRAZER: Oh – the coffee. (*He smiles*) It was a false alarm.

RICHARDS: Really? Are you sure?

FRAZER: Quite sure.

RICHARDS: So Van Dakar was wrong?

FRAZER: (*A shrug*) Perhaps, like Ross, he has a hunch about Barbara Day and wanted me to play safe.

RICHARDS: (*Looking at FRAZER*) Perhaps. (*Suddenly; putting the case on the table*) Well, I've brought what you wanted.

RICHARDS opens the case and takes out the metronome which was taken from DEMPSEY's office.

FRAZER: Good.

RICHARDS: Ross was a bit reluctant about the diamonds …

RICHARDS takes a small jewellery box out of the case.

FRAZER: I thought he might be. But don't worry. I'll take great care of them.

RICHARDS: And here's the other thing you wanted.

RICHARDS takes a gun from the case, and holds it out, butt first, to FRAZER.

FRAZER: Thank you.

117

FRAZER takes the gun and after a brief glance at it puts it in his pocket.

RICHARDS: Dempsey gets to the office about ten. Rarely before then.

FRAZER: Good. That's excellent.

RICHARDS: (*Curious*) Frazer, what exactly are you going to say to Dempsey?

FRAZER: I'm going to tell him a story.

RICHARDS: What story?

FRAZER: (*Smiling; noncommittally*) The one I've got in mind.

RICHARDS: Well, for your sake, I hope it's a good one.

FRAZER: Oh – it's a good one all right. Don't worry about that. Part fact – part fiction. They're always the best stories – aren't they, Richards?

RICHARDS looks a little puzzled.

FRAZER smiles at him then glances down at the metronome.

CUT TO: GORDON DEMPSEY's Office. Long Acre. Day.

A metronome is ticking away on the desk.

After a few moments the office door opens and GORDON DEMPSEY comes in. He makes to move to the desk, stopping dead in his tracks as he sees the metronome. He stares at it; astonished.

FRAZER: (*Out of vision*) Good morning, Mr Dempsey.

DEMPSEY turns sharply. As he does so we see FRAZER seated on a chair facing DEMPSEY. The chair is reversed and FRAZER's arms are on the back of it. He holds the gun, levelled at DEMPSEY.

DEMPSEY: Frazer!

FRAZER nods politely.

DEMPSEY: What do you want?

118

FRAZER rises slowly from the chair.

FRAZER: I just called in to return the metronome.

DEMPSEY half glances at the metronome, then looks back at FRAZER.

DEMPSEY: Why?

FRAZER: Because the significance of it escapes me, Mr Dempsey.

DEMPSEY is silent. He looks warily at the gun in FRAZER's hand.

FRAZER: Sit down.

FRAZER indicates with a nod of the head the chair behind the desk.

DEMPSEY sits in the chair.

FRAZER: I've got something I'd like you to take a look at …

FRAZER produces the box containing the diamonds from his pocket. He opens it, then crosses and puts it down on the desk in front of DEMPSEY.

FRAZER: That's really why I came back. Go on – take a look.

DEMPSEY looks at FRAZER, then down at the open box. He takes out the diamonds. He stares at them, obviously intrigued.

DEMPSEY: Can I – er – (*He indicates the desk drawer*)

FRAZER: Allow me!

FRAZER is not being caught a second time by a gun in the drawer; he opens the drawer. It contains a jeweller's eyeglass. FRAZER takes it out and places it on the desk.

DEMPSEY takes up the glass and carefully examines the diamonds. He puts the eyeglass down after a little while and looks up at FRAZER.

DEMPSEY: Well?

FRAZER: I suppose you want to know where I got them?

119

DEMPSEY: (*Quietly*) You got them off Cordwell.

FRAZER: Yes. I knew Cordwell years ago in America. We were in business together once.

DEMPSEY: What sort of business?

FRAZER: (*Shaking his head*) We won't go into details. I hadn't seen him for several years, then about a week ago I bumped into him in Amsterdam. We had a night out – talked over old times. He was pretty tight, I'm afraid. As soon as he mentioned he was in the diamond business, I knew what he was up to. He used to smuggle drugs across the Canadian border – in a cigar holder.

DEMPSEY: What else did he tell you?

FRAZER: He told me that the organisation he worked for was a fairly large one. He said he always had to contact the head man through several go-betweens – using a bulb catalogue as a means of introduction.

DEMPSEY: Did he mention a name?

FRAZER: Yes, he did. Ericson.

DEMPSEY studies FRAZER. He is evidently still not satisfied with FRAZER's story.

DEMPSEY: You still haven't told me how you got hold of these?

FRAZER: I also met a girl in Amsterdam – Barbara Day. When I got back to London she invited me to her flat for drinks. I went along there and couldn't get an answer. I was just about to go back home when (*He stops*)

DEMPSEY: Go on …

FRAZER: You're not going to believe this, but – (*He shrugs*) Well, if you want to know … I was about to go back home when someone shoved a key under the door from inside. I let myself into the flat and found Cordwell lying there – dead. My first thought, of course, was to beat it, quick. Then I remembered what he'd said about the diamond business. I thought it might be worth while taking a look in his cigar holder. I found it in the fireplace. He must have thrown it there before the struggle. I opened it and lo and behold … (*He indicates the diamonds*)

DEMPSEY looks at the diamonds, then at FRAZER.

DEMPSEY: All right, Frazer, what is it you want?

FRAZER: I want you to get in touch with Ericson and tell him I'm prepared to do a deal.

DEMPSEY: And what makes you think Ericson will be interested?

FRAZER picks up the box containing the diamonds and puts it in his pocket.

FRAZER: Find out. (*He backs to the door*) I'll be in my flat this evening from seven o'clock onwards. (*He opens the door*) But the diamonds won't be – so don't get any bright ideas. Good morning, Mr Dempsey.

FRAZER goes out, closing the door behind him.

DEMPSEY stares after him for a moment, and then looks at the metronome which is still on the desk. Suddenly, he makes a decision, turns, and picks up the telephone. He starts to dial a number.

CUT TO: FRAZER's Drawing Room. Evening.

FRAZER is sitting at the desk, writing a letter. He finishes the letter, then picks up an envelope. Suddenly, with a gesture of impatience, he puts the envelope and pen down on the desk and rises. He crosses to the drinks table and is about to pour himself a drink when the front door bell rings.

FRAZER goes out into the hall and returns with ARTHUR FAIRLEE.

FAIRLEE is obviously distressed.

FRAZER conceals the fact that he is not particularly pleased to see him. He indicates a chair.

FAIRLEE: (*Shaking his head*) No, thank you.

FRAZER: Would you like a drink?

FAIRLEE: No, thank you.

FAIRLEE's tone is faintly hostile. FRAZER looks at him, then returns to the drinks table and continues to mix himself a drink.

FRAZER: Well, you don't mind if I do?

FAIRLEE: Please yourself.

FRAZER: (*Turning; drink in hand*) Well – Fairlee, what's on your mind?

FAIRLEE: I'll tell you what's on my mind …

FRAZER: Please do …

FAIRLEE: Are you having an affair with Barbara?

FRAZER: Am I having … Now, just a minute –

FAIRLEE: Are you?

FRAZER: No, I'm not!

FAIRLEE: Well – she's been seeing a devil of a lot of you just recently, so if you're not having an affair with her why …

FRAZER: (*Stopping FAIRLEE*) Now just a minute! Calm down. (*He faces FAIRLEE; after a moment*) What's this all about? What's happened?

FAIRLEE: You know perfectly well what's happened!

FRAZER: I'm afraid I don't.

FAIRLEE: Barbara's broken off our engagement.

FRAZER: When?

FAIRLEE: Last night.

FRAZER: Oh. Oh, I see.

FAIRLEE: (*Angrily*) Yes, you damn well see all right! You knew perfectly well this was going to happen!

FRAZER: What are you talking about? What the devil do you mean?

FAIRLEE: Everything was all right between us until you came on the scene!

FRAZER: (*Annoyed*) Now listen to me. If Barbara's thrown you over you've got no one to blame but yourself. (*He puts his drink down on the table*) I haven't been having an affair with your fiancée. I haven't even tried. I knew it was no use. She's too damn loyal, Fairlee.

FAIRLEE: (*After a moment*) Is this the truth?

FRAZER: (*Still annoyed*) Of course it's the truth! Good God, man – don't you believe me? You know, you've brought this on yourself. You've taken her too much for granted. Have you ever stopped to think what you've done for Barbara in return for all her kindness? (*Facing FAIRLEE*) Well – have you?

FAIRLEE: When you're not feeling yourself you sometimes – well, you sometimes exaggerate things. Get things out of perspective, as it were.

FRAZER: Yes, I can understand that. I'm sure Barbara understands it, too.

FAIRLEE: (*Contrite*) Oh, she does! She does indeed. She's been wonderful. Really wonderful, Frazer. I can't begin to tell you … (*He stops; looks at FRAZER*) Do you think the breaking off of our engagement was just – well, just a gesture – the mood of the moment?

FRAZER: I don't know. I suppose it could have been. Why don't you ask her?

FAIRLIE looks at FRAZER, then gives a little nod.

FAIRLEE: Yes. Yes, I will. (*After a moment*) I'm sorry, Frazer. I was rude just now …

FRAZER: Oh, forget it …

FAIRLEE: No, I mean it. I was damn rude. I apologise.

FRAZER: All right. Well – in that case, perhaps you'll change your mind about the drink?

FAIRLEE: Yes – may I have a whisky and soda?

FRAZER: Yes, of course.

FRAZER moves towards the drinks table and as he does so the door bell starts to ring.

FRAZER stops and looks towards the hall.

FRAZER: Excuse me. (*Indicating the drinks table*) Help yourself.

FAIRLEE crosses towards the table as FRAZER goes out into the hall.

CUT TO: The Hall.

FRAZER enters from the drawing room and opens the front door.

A TELEGRAM BOY hands him a telegram.

FRAZER slits open the telegram and reads it.

FRAZER: There's no reply.

FRAZER closes the front door and turns towards the drawing room; looking at the telegram again. It reads: "Will meet you eleven o'clock tonight stop park car near Queensmere Pond Wimbledon Dempsey".

FRAZER stares at the telegram. He looks puzzled and distinctly worried.

CUT TO: The Drawing Room.

FRAZER enters, still staring at the telegram.

FAIRLEE looks at him.

FAIRLEE: Not bad news, I hope?

FRAZER: (*Looking up*) No – no, it's just from a friend of
            mine.

CUT TO: Wimbledon Common. Night.
*A section of the road on Wimbledon Common near
Queensmere Pond.*
FRAZER's car drives into shot and stops.
*FRAZER is seated in the driver's seat of his car, surveying the
area.*
A car is heard approaching.
FRAZER watches it.
It drives past, not stopping.
*FRAZER takes out his cigarettes and lights one, preparing to
wait. He looks at his watch.*

CUT TO: Wimbledon Common. Night.
*FRAZER is standing by his car, finishing a cigarette. He looks
at his watch again; making a decision, he throws away his
cigarette, and gets into the car. He starts the engine and the
car drives away.*

CUT TO: Wimbledon Common. Night.
*Shooting through the windscreen of FRAZER's car as it goes
along the road.*
*The headlights illustrate the road. Suddenly a man is seen
leaning against a bicycle in the middle of the road. The man
is a WARDEN of Wimbledon Common and Putney Heath. He
waves a torch, signalling the car to stop.*

CUT TO: Wimbledon Common. Night.
FRAZER's car slows to a standstill.
The WARDEN approaches the car and speaks to FRAZER.

CUT TO: Wimbledon Common. Night.

The WARDEN is talking to FRAZER who is still seated in his car.

WARDEN: ...The man's in a bad way, sir. Otherwise I wouldn't have stopped you.

FRAZER: What is it? What's happened?

FRAZER gets out of the car and walks with the WARDEN to bushes at the roadside through the following dialogue.

WARDEN: Looks like he's had a bit of a beating up to me.

The WARDEN and FRAZER enter the bushes.

The WARDEN leads the way with his torch.

They stop.

The WARDEN indicates a body on the ground.

FRAZER comes abreast of the WARDEN and stares down at the body, recognising it as DEMPSEY's.

DEMPSEY is in a half lying position with his trunk supported on one elbow, his head slumped over.

Hearing the WARDEN and FRAZER approaching he looks up and sees FRAZER, recognising him. He speaks with difficulty ...

DEMPSEY: Hello, Frazer ...

The WARDEN looks surprised that he knows FRAZER.

FRAZER kneels by DEMPSEY.

FRAZER: All right ... Now don't worry, Dempsey, you'll be all right ... we'll take you somewhere and get you patched up ...

The WARDEN helps FRAZER to lift DEMPSEY to his feet. They start to move off in the direction of the car.

DEMPSEY looks at FRAZER.

DEMPSEY: Frazer ...

They stop immediately.

FRAZER: Yes?

DEMPSEY: You ... you should ... (*He finds it difficult to speak*)

FRAZER: What is it, Dempsey?
DEMPSEY: … You should have touched the metronome …
FRAZER looks at DEMPSEY with interest, then they carry on towards the car.

END OF EPISODE FIVE

EPISODE SIX

OPEN TO: Wimbledon Common. Night.

FRAZER and the WARDEN help DEMPSEY towards FRAZER's car which is parked in the road.

They put DEMPSEY in the back seat of the car, then FRAZER gets into the driving seat.

The WARDEN talks to FRAZER through the driving seat window.

WARDEN: Well – I'd better have some particulars. I shall have to report it to the police. If you could just give me his name and address …

FRAZER: (*Cutting the WARDEN short*) Look – I'd better get my friend to hospital. We can leave all that till later.

WARDEN: Oh, it won't take a minute to –

FRAZER: (*Interrupting the WARDEN*) Good night! Thanks for your help!

FRAZER starts his car and drives off.

The WARDEN stares after the departing car.

CUT TO: FRAZER's Drawing Room. Night.

DEMPSEY is seated in an armchair. There is a sticking plaster here and there on his face; he looks much better than he did in the previous scene, but still very much the worse for wear.

He is just finishing a sandwich. On the table before him is a plate of sandwiches and a glass of whisky.

He is in his shirt sleeves, tie and collar loosened. His jacket is on a chair over the other side of the room.

FRAZER is seated, straddled-legged on an upright chair, watching DEMPSEY as he eats the last of his sandwich.

FRAZER: Feeling better now?

DEMPSEY: Yes, a bit.

As if to prove it DEMPSEY starts to rise. Immediately he does so he feels very much worse and slips back into the chair.

131

FRAZER: You'd better stay where you are for a while.
            Now tell me: what did happen out there?

DEMPSEY: I've told you. This gang of kids – yobs –
            attacked me and ...

FRAZER: (*With a note of sarcasm*) And they beat you up
            just for the fun of it?

DEMPSEY: No – they were after my money.

*FRAZER looks at DEMPSEY for a moment, then goes to
DEMPSEY's jacket on the chair. He reaches inside the pocket
and takes out a wallet and a passport. He looks inside the
wallet, then looks at DEMPSEY. He tosses the wallet onto the
table in front of DEMPSEY.*

FRAZER: Seventy pounds or more. They didn't look very
            far, did they?

DEMPSEY: They didn't have time. Must have heard
            someone coming. That warden chap, I suppose.
            Anyway, they all vanished after a yell from one
            of the gang ...

*FRAZER looks at DEMPSEY, obviously not believing this
story. He looks down at the passport in his hands.*

DEMPSEY: (*Watching FRAZER*) That's my passport
            you've got ...

FRAZER: Yes, I can see that, Mr Dempsey.

DEMPSEY, irritated, reaches out for the passport.

FRAZER moves back, putting the passport out of his reach.

DEMPSEY: Look – what the devil are you up to?

*FRAZER looks at DEMPSEY thoughtfully, tapping the
passport lightly on his hand.*

FRAZER: Let me tell you what I think happened.

DEMPSEY: I've told you what happened!

FRAZER: (*Shaking his head*) You wanted the diamonds
            for yourself. This business tonight was a
            warning from Ericson to keep in line.

DEMPSEY is obstinately silent.

132

FRAZER: That's right, isn't it?

DEMPSEY hesitates for a moment, then nods reluctantly.

FRAZER: Who is Ericson?

DEMPSEY: I don't know.

FRAZER looks at DEMPSEY closely.

DEMPSEY's reply seems to be quite genuine.

FRAZER: All right. Tell me what you do know.

DEMPSEY: Why should I do that? You saw what happened to me tonight. If they find out that I've been talking …

FRAZER: Then you'll need this, and the plane ticket for Montreal that's in your wallet.

DEMPSEY looks at FRAZER for a moment with a frightened expression.

FRAZER: You'll need them anyway, Dempsey, because – believe me – this thing's coming to a head.

DEMPSEY: Look, who the hell are you? Who do you represent?

FRAZER: You know who I am. I represent myself. However, let's forget my end of it for a moment, and talk about the Ericson set-up.

DEMPSEY: I don't know anything about the Ericson set-up.

FRAZER: I think you do. I think you know a great deal about it.

FRAZER sits on the arm of the settee.

FRAZER: The diamonds are stolen on the Continent and brought to this country by people like Cordwell; then by various means they're passed on to Ericson.

FRAZER looks at DEMPSEY for confirmation.

FRAZER: In short: if I was working for Ericson, then my first step would be to go to The Amstel coffee bar, produce the catalogue, and be passed on to you. That's right, isn't it?

133

DEMPSEY: (*After a moment; nodding*) Yes, that's right.

FRAZER: Now tell me the rest …

DEMPSEY: Why the hell should I?

FRAZER: Because if you don't – you don't get this, Mr Dempsey. (*He holds up the passport*) It's as simple as that.

DEMPSEY looks at FRAZER; he is obviously a very worried man.

FRAZER: Go on, Dempsey.

DEMPSEY: When you get through to me I ask for the code word …

FRAZER: Fantasy …

DEMPSEY: (*Nodding*) That's right, but it's changed every week. If you give the correct code word then there's one more test.

FRASER: The metronome?

DEMPSEY: Yes. You remember I put it on the desk in front of you?

FRAZER nods.

DEMPSEY: I was waiting for you to move the lead indicator to a particular number on the metronome scale.

FRAZER: I see.

DEMPSEY: Like the code word, the number's changed every week.

FRAZER: So it's pretty impossible for an imposter to get through?

DEMPSEY: Yes …

FRAZER: Well – supposing I'd known the number? What then?

DEMPSEY: I'd have passed you on to someone else.

FRAZER: Who? Ericson?

DEMPSEY: No.

FRAZER: (*Suddenly*) Vivien Gilmore?

DEMPSEY: (*Taken aback*) Yes – yes; that's right. How did you know?

FRAZER: (*Dismissing the matter*) Miss Gilmore happens to be a friend of a friend of mine. (*Leaning forward*) But tell me: what would she do? Pay me off and pass the diamonds over to Ericson?

DEMPSEY: (*After a momentary hesitation*) Yes …

FRAZER: You don't seem very sure of that?

DEMPSEY: I'm not … Miss Gilmore's activities are no concern of mine.

FRAZER watches DEMPSEY for a moment, then rises from the settee.

FRAZER: Dempsey, a man called Leo Salinger was killed in a car accident in Amsterdam. He was carrying a metronome at the time.

DEMPSEY: Yes, I know. The metronome contained stolen diamonds. He was bringing them to England.

FRAZER: You mean Leo Salinger was working for Ericson?

DEMPSEY: (*Hesitating*) No – but his brother, Arnold, was. He received stolen diamonds and frequently brought them to England. After a big haul, Arnold fell ill and couldn't bring them over. His brother, Leo, happened to be coming to England, so Arnold hit on the idea of concealing the diamonds in the metronome and getting Leo to deliver them.

FRAZER: And Leo knew nothing about the diamonds?

DEMPSEY: As far as he was concerned he was just delivering a birthday present to a friend of his brother's.

FRAZER: I see.

DEMPSEY: But Leo Salinger never got here with the metronome. He never even left Amsterdam. He was killed in a car accident on the way to the airport – and the metronome disappeared. Ericson, of course, was angry, intensely angry, about the whole affair. I think he thought Arnold was trying to double cross him.

FRAZER: What happened?

DEMPSEY: He put pressure on the poor devil and Arnold finished up by committing suicide.

FRAZER: But how do you propose Cordwell got hold of the missing diamonds?

DEMPSEY: I don't know. Cordwell was in the diamond racket, of course, and must have known that Leo was carrying the diamonds. He was probably following Leo at the time. The rest you know. Cordwell came over here, tried to do a deal with Ericson, and was murdered.

FRAZER: Why?

DEMPSEY: I don't know why. Your guess is as good as mine.

FRAZER: I doubt that.

FRAZER turns the pages of the passport and looks at the photograph; quietly.

FRAZER: I doubt that very much, Mr Dempsey.

There is a pause.

FRAZER looks up at DEMPSEY.

DEMPSEY: Well – my guess is Ericson was angry with Cordwell because he'd discovered his identity and insisted on dealing with him direct. But that's only my guess, of course.

DEMPSEY looks at the passport in FRAZER's hand.

DEMPSEY: Well – do I get my passport, Mr Frazer?

FRAZER looks at DEMPSEY, hesitates.

DEMPSEY watches FRAZER with a distinctly worried expression.

After a moment, and with an effort, he rises, and moves down towards FRAZER.

FRAZER looks at the passport again, then at DEMPSEY.

FRAZER: I should change the photograph, Mr Dempsey. You look most untrustworthy.

FRAZER throws the passport across to DEMPSEY.

CUT TO: The Amstel Coffee Bar. Day.

VIVIEN is sitting at a table. After a moment JAN puts a cup of coffee down in front of her. There is no one else in the coffee bar.

JAN: He's late.

VIVIEN: Yes.

JAN: Do you think he'll come?

VIVIEN: Of course he'll come. He said he would.

JAN: This was last night?

VIVIEN: Yes, I've told you. I telephoned him.

JAN: What time was that?

VIVIEN: When I phoned him? About a quarter to twelve.

JAN: And he said he'd be here at ten-thirty?

VIVIEN: I <u>told</u> him to be here at ten-thirty. Stop worrying!

JAN: Yes – well, my bet is, he won't come.

The café door opens and FRAZER enters.

VIVIEN: It looks as if you've lost your bet already.

VIVIEN looks at FRAZER. She is suddenly tense; hard and businesslike.

VIVIEN: All right. I want the Cordwell diamonds.

FRAZER: (*Apparently puzzled*) Diamonds?

VIVIEN: Let's not play games, Mr Frazer. I know you've got them.

FRAZER: I'm sorry, but I'm afraid I don't know what you're talking about.

VIVIEN gives a little sigh of impatience and looks across at JAN. He nods to VIVIEN then starts a tape recorder which is concealed below the bar counter.

After a moment voices are heard from the tape recorder.

DEMPSEY's VOICE: Well, how ... What would you like to order? Which ones do you want?

FRAZER's VOICE: I – er – haven't quite made up my mind ...

DEMPSEY's VOICE: I see. Well – we've got Piccadilly, Red Parrot, Fantasy, Octavius, Hilversum Red ...

FRAZER's VOICE: I'd like some Fantasy.

DEMPSEY's VOICE: How many?

FRAZER's VOICE: Oh – I should say – two-thirty ...

DEMPSEY's VOICE: All right, Mr Scott ...

FRAZER is staring in the direction of the bar.

VIVIEN smiles faintly.

FRAZER looks at her.

FRAZER: So you didn't trust Dempsey?

VIVIEN: Ericson didn't, but then he doesn't trust anyone, not even me.

VIVIEN nods to JAN. He switches off the tape recorder. She looks back at FRAZER.

FRAZER: All right. What's he prepared to pay?

VIVIEN: (*Coldly*) He's not prepared to pay anything, Mr Frazer. He just wants them.

FRAZER: Oh, now look, you're a business woman ...

VIVIEN: I've got my instructions in this matter. I do as I'm told. You hand over the diamonds – and that's all there is to it.

FRAZER: As simple as that?

VIVIEN: Yes. If you don't hand them over we shall tell the police that you've got them. That, coupled

138

with the fact that they found your fingerprints on the door of Barbara's flat …

FRAZER: (*Interrupting VIVIEN*) Now wait a minute! The police have got to find the diamonds. I doubt very much if they'd just take your word for it …

VIVIEN: Frazer, don't be a fool! You saw what happened to Dempsey.

FRAZER: Yes, I saw – but I'm afraid you're overlooking something.

VIVIEN: What's that?

FRAZER: I'm not Dempsey.

FRAZER rises from the table.

FRAZER: Tell Ericson I'll take forty thousand. They're worth a great deal more than that – but I'll settle for forty.

VIVIEN: (*Shaking her head*) He won't pay that.

FRAZER: (*Smiling*) Well, deliver the message, anyway. Goodbye, Vivien.

FRAZER goes to the door.

VIVIEN glares after him.

FRAZER opens the door, turns the "Closed" sign around to "Open", glances fleetingly at VIVIEN, and goes.

VIVIEN looks across at JAN with a set expression.

CUT TO: FRAZER's Drawing Room. Day.

FRAZER and BARBARA DAY have been having a cup of tea together. He is sitting on the settee, smoking a cigarette, and watching BARBARA as she rises from the armchair and puts an empty teacup down on the tea trolley.

FRAZER: …Well, I'll say this for you, Barbara, this is the first time you've been here without saying, "I must fly – Vivien's waiting."

BARBARA laughs.

139

BARBARA: I was just going to say it. (*Glancing at her watch; surprised*) My goodness, so I really must fly! Thanks for the tea.

FRAZER rises.

FRAZER: Thanks for coming.

BARBARA picks up her handbag and gloves from the settee. FRAZER watches her.

FRAZER: (*Quietly*) Barbara …

BARBARA: (*Turning*) Yes?

FRAZER: You've been here almost an hour …

BARBARA: Well?

FRAZER: And you still haven't told me why you came.

BARBARA looks at FRAZER; hesitates.

FRAZER: You've broken off your engagement – haven't you?

BARBARA: (*Astonished*) Why – yes! How did you know?

FRAZER: Arthur told me. He came to see me.

BARBARA: (*Moving down to FRAZER; amazed*) Arthur came to see you?

FRAZER: Yes.

BARBARA: Why?

FRAZER: Well – I suppose he just wanted to talk to someone.

BARBARA: Did he blame you – for what's happened, I mean?

FRAZER: (*Hesitantly*) Well …

BARBARA: Did he, Tim?

FRAZER: (*Smiling*) Yes, he did – but I'm afraid I wouldn't stand for it.

BARBARA: Good. I'm glad to hear that. I realise now it was a mistake. I should never have got engaged to him in the first place.

FRAZER: Well – it's over now.

BARBARA: I don't know …

FRAZER looks at BARBARA closely.

BARBARA: Arthur phoned me this morning – in a terrible state. He threatened to commit suicide if I didn't go back to him.

FRAZER: Look – I know threats like that can be very worrying, but I think you've got to stick to your guns over this. Otherwise you're merely going to end up like you were before; Arthur phoning you up every five minutes and you rushing round there to look after him.

BARBARA: But I'm frightened that he …

FRAZER: He won't go through with it, don't worry. You take my word for it. I warn you, Barbara, if you give in now you'll end up marrying him!

BARBARA: Well – what do you think I should do?

FRAZER: If I were you I'd go away for a little while. Let him get used to the fact that he's got to stand on his own feet from now on.

BARBARA: Yes, actually, I've been thinking about that – getting away, I mean.

FRAZER: (*Nodding*) It's the only answer.

BARBARA: The trouble is it's so difficult at the moment. Vivien's got a big deal on and I can't possibly just walk out and leave her to it.

FRAZER: I see. (*He looks thoughtful*) How long have you known Vivien?

BARBARA: Oh, just over two years now. Arthur introduced us – I think I told you.

FRAZER: What did she do before you met her?

BARBARA: I don't really know. I think she was in some sort of business or other. She never seems very keen on talking about the past. Why?

141

FRAZER: I just wondered, that's all. Look – about Arthur – if you can't get away, then you've simply got to refuse to see him.

BARBARA: Yes, all right.

FRAZER: You've got to be tough about it, Barbara.

BARBARA: Yes, I suppose I have. (*Smiling, gratefully*) Well – thanks, Tim. You've been very kind. And, believe me, I do appreciate it. I really shouldn't bother you like this …

FRAZER: …Nonsense …

BARBARA: … You've got troubles of your own, I'm sure. (*Putting on her gloves*) Vivien was saying that you're not doing too well at the moment.

FRAZER: (*A shade irritated*) Vivien talks too much. Oh, I'm doing all right, I suppose – but I'm afraid I was never meant to earn my living as a journalist. As far as I'm concerned the piston ring is mightier than the pen.

BARBARA: Well, why don't you try and get back into engineering?

FRAZER: I'm going to – as soon as I can find the necessary capital.

BARBARA: How much do you need?

FRAZER: Oh – about forty thousand. (*Smiling*) It's a tidy sum, but I'll find it all right.

BARBARA: Why are you smiling?

FRAZER: I was just thinking; at one time I thought of trying to borrow it from your fiancé.

BARBARA: (*Amused*) I don't think you'd have had much success at the moment.

FRAZER and BARBARA go out into the hall.

CUT TO: The Hall.

FRAZER: No, I'm sure I wouldn't … (*He faces BARBARA*) Barbara, when am I going to see you again?

BARBARA: Well, I don't know, perhaps … (*She hesitates, then:*) Would you like to come to my place tonight – after dinner?

FRAZER: I'll think it over. Yes.

BARBARA laughs.

BARBARA: Well – let's say nine o'clock.

FRAZER: That's fine.

BARBARA: See you then. Goodbye.

FRAZER opens the door and BARBARA goes out.

He closes the door and stands for a moment in the hall, thinking about the invitation.

CUT TO: FRAZER's Drawing Room. Night.

LEWIS RICHARDS is sitting in an armchair, holding a glass of brandy.

RICHARDS: Well – Ross is certainly going to be interested in your little talk with Dempsey. It means that Leo Salinger was in the clear.

FRAZER: Yes. Incidentally, Dempsey was puzzled by the fact that Leo's metronome was missing.

RICHARDS: I expect he was. We had a man tailing Leo because we weren't sure of him. He picked up the metronome.

FRAZER: But the metronome didn't contain the diamonds.

RICHARDS: No; Cordwell evidently found out about Arnold Salinger's plan for sending the diamonds to London and made a switch. It wouldn't be difficult, of course, since Leo didn't know anything about the diamonds.

143

FRAZER nods.

RICHARDS: Incidentally, I saw Van Dakar this morning.

FRAZER: How is he?

RICHARDS: A lot better. We had a long talk. He's a private investigator for one of the Dutch insurance companies. He's been on to this Ericson set-up for some time. He got as far as Dempsey, then came to a dead stop.

FRAZER: I suppose he was wondering where I fitted in?

RICHARDS: (*Nodding*) That's why he searched your flat. He'd watched you going into Barbara Day's flat the night Cordwell was murdered and thought you'd got hold of the diamonds.

FRAZER: If he thought that why did he give me the tip about the Amstel coffee bar and the code word Fantasy?

RICHARDS: When he couldn't find the diamonds in your flat, he came round to Lloyd's idea about you.

FRAZER: Lloyd?

RICHARDS: Van Dakar's assistant – the man who was with him.

FRAZER nods understandingly.

RICHARDS: He thought you were an Interpol man. Van Dakar decided to take a chance and let you in on what they already knew.

FRAZER: I see.

RICHARDS: You've done a good job, Frazer. So far as we're concerned this business is over. Leo Salinger was innocent – that's all Ross wanted to know.

FRAZER: Yes – well, it's not over so far as I'm concerned.

RICHARDS: What do you mean?

FRAZER: What happens to the diamonds?

RICHARDS: Van Dakar takes them back to Holland.

FRAZER: When?

RICHARDS: When he gets a clearance from the Yard; probably at the end of the week. (*A pause: he is looking at FRAZER*) There's something on your mind, Frazer. What is it?

Another pause.

FRAZER: Richards, do you think you could get me some imitation diamonds? I mean – really first class imitations?

RICHARDS: I could try. I could have a word with Ross about it. He can manage most things. But what's the point?

FRAZER: Vivien Gilmore thinks I've got the diamonds. It's my bet she's going to make an appointment for me to see Ericson.

RICHARDS: But we're not interested in Ericson.

FRAZER: No, but I am! I'm very interested in Ericson. Besides, when I start a job I like to finish it. I'm finishing this one.

FRAZER holds out his hand for RICHARDS' empty glass.

RICHARDS rises, hands over his glass, and watches FRAZER as he goes over to the drinks table.

RICHARDS shakes his head with a faintly worried expression as much as to say "It's your own funeral, old man."

CUT TO: BARBARA DAY's Flat. Night.

BARBARA is sitting at her desk turning over the pages of her engagement book; studying the entries. She finally picks up the book and takes it to VIVIEN GILMORE who is sitting on the settee.

BARBARA: … If I do get away for a few days, say on Tuesday …

VIVIEN: Take the whole week off, Barbara. It's just silly going away for a few days. You need a complete break after all this nonsense with Arthur.

BARBARA: (*Looking at her diary*) We're supposed to be going out to Brighton on Thursday. There's that big sale ...

VIVIEN: Forget it, Barbara. I can deal with Brighton ...

The telephone rings.

BARBARA crosses to the phone.

As she picks up the receiver the front door bell is heard ringing.

BARBARA looks across at VIVIEN.

BARBARA: (*On the phone*) Hello? ... Oh! Just a minute, Arthur!

VIVIEN: It's all right. I'll get it.

VIVIEN goes into the hall.

CUT TO: The Hall of BARBARA DAY's Flat.

VIVIEN goes to the front door and opens it.

FRAZER is in the doorway.

VIVIEN: Oh – good evening! Do come in! Barbara's on the phone.

FRAZER: Thank you.

FRAZER is evidently surprised to see VIVIEN. He comes into the hall.

VIVIEN closes the front door and leads FRAZER into the living room.

CUT TO: The Living Room.

VIVIEN and FRAZER enter; BARBARA is still on the phone.

She looks up, seeing FRAZER. She covers the mouthpiece of the receiver.

BARBARA: Oh – hello, Tim! Would you excuse me a moment? (*On the phone*) Just hold on … (*Offering VIVIEN the receiver*) Vivien, do you mind? I'll take it in the bedroom.

VIVIEN takes the receiver.

BARBARA: (*To FRAZER*) I shan't be a moment. (*To VIVIEN*) Give Tim a drink, would you?

BARBARA goes into the bedroom.

VIVIEN waits until she hears BARBARA's voice on the line, from the bedroom, then she puts down the receiver.

VIVIEN: Do sit down.

FRAZER: (*Quietly; looking at VIVIEN*) Thank you.

VIVIEN: (*Indicating the telephone*) I don't have to tell you who that is …

FRAZER: Fairlee?

VIVIEN: Yes. He keeps ringing her night and day. (*Turning towards the drinks table*) What would you like to drink?

FRAZER: Nothing, just at the moment. I'll wait for Barbara.

A pause.

VIVIEN: I was going to phone you, anyway – then Barbara said you were coming here. I have some news for you. (*A pause*) I've spoken to Ericson.

FRAZER is looking at VIVIEN, interested.

FRAZER: Well?

VIVIEN looks towards the bedroom door in a listening attitude, then looks back at FRAZER.

VIVIEN: We can't talk now. Could you meet me later?

FRAZER: Tonight?

VIVIEN: Yes.

FRAZER: Yes, I could. Where?

VIVIEN: Did you come in your car?

FRAZER: No, a taxi.

VIVIEN: Then I'll pick you up when you leave here.

FRAZER: Is Ericson interested?

VIVIEN: (*Turning away from FRAZER; softly*) I'll tell you later.

FRAZER is about to speak when the bedroom door opens and BARBARA returns. She looks a little upset.

FRAZER rises as she enters.

BARBARA: I'm sorry about that.

FRAZER: That's all right.

VIVIEN: Well, dear, I'll be on my way.

BARBARA: Oh, please don't dash off because of Tim.

VIVIEN: (*Smiling faintly*) Don't bother being polite, Barbara. I know when I'm not wanted.

BARBARA: (*Faintly embarrassed*) Vivien …

VIVIEN: I've got things to do, anyway. Don't, please! I'll see myself out … Good night, Mr Frazer.

FRAZER: Good night.

FRAZER and VIVIEN's eyes hold fleetingly.

VIVIEN goes out.

FRAZER looks at BARBARA, waiting for her to speak.

FRAZER: You look tired.

BARBARA: Yes, I am rather.

FRAZER: Was that Arthur?

BARBARA nods.

FRAZER: What did you say?

BARBARA: I said I couldn't see him.

FRAZER: Good for you!

BARBARA: He's trying every trick in the book. He even got his doctor to phone this morning to say he mustn't be subjected to nervous strain and anxiety.

FRAZER: I hope you gave the doctor a piece of your mind.

148

BARBARA: Well, I wasn't very polite, I'm afraid. Anyway, I'm sure you didn't come here to talk about Arthur. Didn't Vivien offer you a drink?

FRAZER: Yes, she did, but I said I'd wait for you. Could I have a Scotch?

BARBARA: Yes, of course.

BARBARA crosses to the drinks table.

BARBARA: Soda?

FRAZER: No, straight, if you don't mind.

BARBARA: I've decided to take your advice, Tim. I'm going away; having a holiday.

FRAZER: I'm delighted to hear it. Where are you going?

BARBARA: I haven't really made up my mind. I thought I'd talk to you about it. (*Turning*) I did think of Scotland. I haven't been there for some time, and I'm very fond of it.

FRAZER: Yes, so am I. What part of Scotland were you thinking of?

BARBARA takes the drink across to him.

BARBARA: I thought I might stay in Edinburgh. It's a very good centre.

FRAZER: (*Taking the drink*) It is indeed.

BARBARA: You like it?

FRAZER looks at BARBARA for a moment; then smiles.

FRAZER: It's my favourite city.

BARBARA: (*After a moment; looking at FRAZER*) I was hoping you'd say that.

CUT TO: Cheyne Walk. Chelsea. London. Night.

FRAZER is strolling along on the lookout for VIVIEN's car.
He stops on seeing the car and crosses the road.
VIVIEN's car is parked at the kerb.
She waves to FRAZER from the driving seat.
FRAZER gets into the car.

VIVIEN starts the car and drives off.

CUT TO: Inside VIVIEN's Car. Night.
VIVIEN is driving the car; FRAZER sitting beside her.
VIVIEN is a shade tense, on edge.
VIVIEN: I've spoken to Ericson. He's prepared to do a deal.
FRAZER: And what does that mean exactly?
VIVIEN: You said you wanted forty thousand …
FRAZER: That's right.
VIVIEN: He'll pay you forty. Bring the diamonds to a house in Maida Vale.
FRAZER: A house in Maida Vale?
VIVIEN: Yes – those are my instructions.
FRAZER: (*Watching VIVIEN*) Where is this house in Maida Vale?
VIVIEN: It's 3 Monkton Villas. We'll expect you tomorrow afternoon at four o'clock.
FRAZER: 3 Monkton Villas?
VIVIEN: Yes.
VIVIEN takes a Yale key from out of her glove compartment and hands it to FRAZER.
VIVIEN: There's a For Sale sign outside the house. You can let yourself in and wait for us in case we're not on time.
FRAZER looks at VIVIEN; obviously considering her instructions.
FRAZER: What guarantee have I that I'll come out of the house with the money – and in one piece, for that matter?
VIVIEN: You've no guarantee, Mr Frazer. You don't have to come if you don't want to.
FRAZER: (*After a moment*) I'll be there.

150

VIVIEN: (*Looking at FRAZER*) And alone, if you don't
            mind.

*FRAZER nods, puts the key in his pocket, and looks ahead
down the road.*

FRAZER: You can drop me on the next corner.

The car slows down.

FRAZER puts his hand on the door handle. He hesitates.

FRAZER: Oh, Vivien …

VIVIEN: Yes?

FRAZER: When I get back to my flat I'm going to write a
            letter. I shall address it to Inspector Trueman.
            Tomorrow morning I shall hand it over to my
            bank manager with very definite instructions.
            I'm sure I don't have to tell you what those
            instructions are. If anything goes wrong in the
            afternoon, he'll deliver it to Scotland Yard –
            personally. Good night, Vivien.

The car has stopped now.

FRAZER gets out and slams the door shut.

VIVIEN sits there, glaring after him.

CUT TO: FRAZER's Drawing Room. Day.

*LEWIS RICHARDS is holding the key that VIVIEN gave to
FRAZER. He takes a small pad – rather like a damp ink pad
for rubber stamps – out of his pocket, and takes an impression
of the key. He puts the pad back in his pocket.*

*An exceedingly impatient FRAZER is standing near the settee
watching RICHARDS.*

RICHARDS crosses to the settee and gives FRAZER the key.

RICHARDS: Thanks. It's all yours now. And the best of
            luck!

FRAZER puts the key in his waistcoat pocket.

RICHARDS: I'm glad it's your neck and not mine.

151

FRASER: It certainly will be my neck if I've got nothing
            to give Ericson for the forty thousand.

RICHARDS: Ah, yes.

RICHARDS sits on the arm of the settee.

RICHARDS: I saw Ross. I told him what you said and what
            you intended to do.

FRAZER: Well?

RICHARDS: He was delighted with the news about Salinger.
            He and Leo were great friends, you know.

FRAZER: (*Impatiently*) Yes, I rather gather that.

RICHARDS: On top of which Ross rather prides himself on
            his choice of men. It wouldn't have done him
            much good if Leo'd turned out to be working
            for Ericson.

FRAZER: Look, Richards – get to the point! What did he
            say about the diamonds?

RICHARDS: The diamonds? Oh, yes, yes, of course!

*RICHARDS reaches inside his pocket and produces a
jewellery box. He hands it to FRAZER.*

*FRAZER looks at the box for a moment, taken aback. He
opens it and sees the diamonds.*

FRAZER: (*Astonished*) Are these the copies – the
            imitations?

RICHARDS: Yes.

FRAZER: But they're fabulous! I can't tell them from the
            real ones!

RICHARDS: (*Quietly*) Let's hope your friends are of the
            same opinion.

CUT TO: A Cul-de-sac in Maida Vale. Day.

*A small, deserted cul-de-sac, with old-fashioned houses in a
bad state of repair.*

*FRAZER's car stops on the corner of the street and FRAZER
gets out.*

He stands beside the car and looks down the street.
He starts to walk down the street, looking up at the numbers of the houses.
He stops outside Number 3. It has a For Sale sign outside it, with a local agent's name on the board.
FRAZER walks up to the front door and rings the bell.
He continues ringing it – but there is no reply.
After a moment he takes out the Yale key, inserts it in the lock, and pushes open the door.
FRAZER enters the house.

CUT TO: Inside Number 3, Monkton Villas. Maida Vale. The Hall of the House. Day.
FRAZER comes in through the front door, closes it behind him, and remains there for a moment, looking around the dusty, gloomy hall.
After a few moments he moves towards the living room door.
He hesitates at the closed door, then, with a sudden cautious movement, throws it open.
He stares into the room.

CUT TO: The Living Room of the House.
Most of the furniture is covered with dust sheets. There is a writing bureau and a table which are uncovered.
FRAZER walks slowly into the room.
He listens for a moment, as if hearing something.
He looks at his watch, checking the time.
He looks thoughtful for a moment, then starts to look around the room.
He walks round the settee and stops abruptly, looking down at the floor.
It is the body of DEMPSEY.

FRAZER kneels quickly by the body and feels DEMPSEY's heart. It is obvious from FRAZER's expression that DEMPSEY is dead.

The telephone starts to ring.

FRAZER is startled by the noise of the bell.

He rises sharply, looking about him for the telephone.

He sees it on top of the writing bureau.

Covering his hand with his handkerchief, he crosses to the phone and takes up the receiver.

LEWIS RICHARDS is heard at the other end of the line. We do not see him during this telephone conversation.

RICHARDS: (*On the other end; tensely*) Is that you, Frazer?

FRAZER: (*Taken aback*) Yes – who is that?

RICHARDS: It's Richards. Frazer, listen! This is important, desperately important! Return to your flat! At once! You understand? Return at once – it's urgent!

We hear the click of the receiver being replaced at the other end.

FRAZER stares at the receiver in his hand, then across at the body of DEMPSEY.

CUT TO: FRAZER's Flat. Day.

FRAZER's car drives up and stops outside the entrance to the flat.

FRAZER gets out and rushes towards the entrance.

CUT TO: The Hall of FRAZER's Flat. Day.

FRAZER comes in through the front door, closes it, and crosses quickly to the drawing room.

CUT TO: The Drawing Room. Day.

FRAZER enters and looks around the room.

154

He is puzzled; everything appears to be perfectly normal; nothing disturbed.

He slowly takes off his hat and coat and drops them onto a chair.

He looks at the telephone, crosses to it, and puts his hand on the receiver.

He finally changes his mind about making the call and goes across to the drinks table where he mixes himself a drink.

He raises the glass to his lips, then freezes, hearing a sound behind him.

He swings around looking towards the bedroom.

He sees someone in the bedroom doorway and a look of great surprise comes over his face.

He lowers his eyes a little – the person is obviously pointing a gun at him.

FRAZER: I didn't know you carried a gun …

END OF EPISODE SIX

EPISODE SEVEN

OPEN TO: The Living Room of Number 3, Monkton Villas. Maida Vale. Day.

FRAZER slowly puts down his glass and raises his hands above his head.

We now see that the person is ARTHUR FAIRLEE, gun in hand, facing FRAZER from the bedroom doorway.

This is a slightly different FAIRLEE from the one we have become accustomed to seeing; much less vague and ill-looking, a comparatively determined looking man.

FRAZER: What's all this about? If you're looking for Barbara …

FAIRLEE: I'm not looking for Barbara. You know why I'm here, Frazer. Hand them over.

FRAZER: (*Ignoring the demand*) I had an appointment with Vivien this afternoon. Why didn't she keep it?

FAIRLEE: We had trouble with Dempsey.

Moving towards FRAZER.

FAIRLEE: Frazer, I haven't a lot of time.

FRAZER: All right … (*He puts his hand in his pocket*) But the price is forty thousand. I told Vivien that.

FAIRLEE: (*Angrily*) I'm not interested in what you told Vivien. You're in no position to bargain, Frazer. Wasn't Dempsey a warning to you?

FRAZER: My dear chap, if I took any notice of warnings I'd have come to a full stop when I found Cordwell.

FAIRLEE: Cordwell was a fool; he wasn't content with selling the diamonds; he had to go in for blackmail.

FRAZER: Yes, I know. But if I give you the diamonds what guarantee have I got that I won't end up like Dempsey?

159

FAIRLEE: You've no guarantee.

FRAZER: Then what's the point of my giving them to you?

ARTHUR FAIRLEE's expression hardens. He levels the gun ominously at FRAZER.

FAIRLEE: The point is very simple. If you don't give them to me you will finish up like Dempsey. Here – and now!

FAIRLEE cocks the gun.

FRAZER sees that he intends to shoot.

FRAZER: (*Quietly*) All right …

FRAZER takes the small jewellery box out of his pocket and holds it out to FAIRLEE.

FAIRLEE: Open it!

FRAZER hesitates for a second, then opens the box showing the diamonds to FAIRLEE.

He tilts the box as he extends his arm.

One of the diamonds falls to the floor.

FRAZER: I'm sorry …

FRAZER bends to pick up the fallen diamond.

As he does so he flings the box containing the other diamonds into ARTHUR FAIRLEE's face.

This distracts FAIRLEE's concentration enough to enable FRAZER to come up from the floor under FAIRLEE's gun arm and seize hold of it.

He twists the gun with a violent movement and the gun is flung across the room.

FAIRLEE lashes out at FRAZER with his free arm,

FRAZER evades the blow and closes with FAIRLEE.

They grapple together, both looking in the direction of the gun to locate its position on the floor.

FRAZER heaves FAIRLEE away from him and dives for the gun on the floor.

He reaches it and picks it up.

160

He makes to turn to face FAIRLEE just as FAIRLEE jumps on top of him in an attempt to wrench the gun from him.

Having the advantage of being behind FRAZER and pulling FRAZER's arm backwards, FAIRLEE manages to free the gun from FRAZER's grasp and takes possession of it.

He points it at the back of FRAZER's neck. He jabs it viciously into the flesh.

FRAZER winces.

One feels ARTHUR FAIRLEE will fire the gun at any moment.

A hand, holding another gun, comes into shot and crashes down on FAIRLEE's head.

FAIRLEE slumps to the floor, unconscious.

FRAZER twists around and looks up at his unseen saviour.

He smiles faintly recognising RICHARDS.

FRAZER scrambles to his feet.

RICHARDS looks down at ARTHUR FAIRLEE's unconscious body.

FRAZER: Thanks.

RICHARDS: It's a pleasure.

RICHARDS puts his gun back into his pocket.

RICHARDS: Doesn't do too badly for a sick man, does he?

FRAZER rubs the back of his neck ruefully, then looks down at FAIRLEE.

FRAZER: Well – this time he'll really need a doctor!

RICHARDS smiles, goes to the telephone, and takes up the receiver. He starts to dial.

CUT TO: Outside Victoria Station. London. Day.

A taxi drives up and stops outside the entrance to the station.

BARBARA DAY gets out of the taxi.

A PORTER arrives and takes her suitcase.

BARBARA pays the driver and the taxi moves off.

BARBARA follows the PORTER into the station.

CUT TO: Inside Victoria Station. Day.

Outside the buffet room on the main platform.

BARBARA and the PORTER walk up to the buffet.

PORTER: Platform 7, miss. But you've got bags of time yet.

The PORTER looks in the direction of the station clock.

PORTER: Let's see – twenty-six minutes. So if you want a cup o' tea or anythin' …

BARBARA: Thank you.

PORTER: I'll see you on the platform, miss.

THE PORTER nods and goes.

BARBARA goes into the buffet.

CUT TO: Outside Victoria Station. London. Day.

A taxi draws up and FRAZER jumps out, pays the driver, and goes into the station.

CUT TO: Station Buffet. Victoria Station. Day.

BARBARA is seated alone at a table, smoking a cigarette. She has a half-finished drink on the table before her.

She glances casually at the people coming in and out of the lounge.

Suddenly FRAZER appears.

BARBARA is obviously expecting him and she smiles as he approaches her.

BARBARA: Well, hello! So you made it!

FRAZER: Yes, I made it.

BARBARA: Am I glad to see you! I had a horrible feeling you were going to let me down.

FRAZER: I told you I'd join you unless you heard from me.

BARBARA: Yes, I know, but I've been involved in so many panics just lately. Incidentally, the plane's delayed, they've just announced it.

A pause.

BARBARA is puzzled by FRAZER's manner.

BARBARA: Aren't you going to sit down?

FRAZER: Barbara, I've got a confession to make. I didn't come here just to go away with you. I have another reason, a very important reason, for being here. I'm meeting someone …

BARBARA: (*Puzzled*) Meeting someone? Who? Who are you meeting, Tim?

FRAZER: Ericson …

BARBARA: Ericson?

FRAZER: Yes … Arthur Fairlee's made a full statement to the police. They know about the diamonds and why Cordwell came to see you. They know how Fairlee murdered him, then pushed the key under the door so that I could let myself into the flat and leave my fingerprints.

BARBARA: (*Tensely*) Go on …

FRAZER: You both went down the fire escape – then you came back through the front door and put on one of your most convincing performances.

BARBARA: I'm glad you found it convincing.

FRAZER: Oh, I did. I did, indeed, Barbara. But tell me: why did you invite me to your flat that night?

BARBARA: So that Arthur could take a look at you. I knew you'd been following me in Amsterdam and I thought he'd recognise you if you were in the diamond business.

FRAZER: So there was no intention of murdering Cordwell in the first place?

BARBARA: No. He turned up out of the blue. Fortunately, as it happened, it all worked out rather well.

FRAZER: Except for the diamonds …

BARBARA: Yes – except for the diamonds. (*Looking at FRAZER*) What made you think of looking for that cigar holder?

FRAZER: It's my job to look for things like that. (*Quietly*) You killed Salinger and you involved your fiancé and your best friend in this business. (*Facing BARBARA*) You're Ericson, aren't you, Barbara?

BARBARA: (*After a pause*) Yes, I'm Ericson.

BARBARA stares at FRAZER for a long while; there is a peculiar intensity in her look.

FRAZER hesitates, then goes towards the exit.

BARBARA sits for a moment, staring at FRAZER's departing figure, then she suddenly pulls herself together, looks at her watch, and moves to pick up her handbag.

As her hand reaches the bag a shadow falls across her and she quickly turns – to find INSPECTOR TRUEMAN and a plain-clothes detective standing by the table.

CUT TO: The Library. 29 Marsham Square. London. Day.

CHARLES ROSS is sitting behind his desk. On the desk are the two cameras belonging to FRAZER and CORDWELL.

FRAZER is seated on the other side of the desk, and RICHARDS is standing nearby.

FRAZER: … Yes, well I don't expect you to believe me but I'd had my eye on her for some time. Then when I got back to my flat yesterday afternoon and found Fairlee there the whole thing clicked. (*Suddenly, to RICHARDS*) Incidentally, you telephoned me – just after I found Dempsey's body …

RICHARDS: Yes, I did.

FRAZER: How did you get the phone number?

ROSS: Mr Frazer, this department is not a suicide squad. We like to play safe – within reason. Since you insisted on keeping your appointment with Ericson I asked Richards to have a look over the house beforehand.

RICHARDS: I made a note of the phone number.

FRAZER: Then when you told me to go back to my flat you knew that Fairlee was there?

RICHARDS: Yes. I had a feeling someone might turn up and search the flat – to try and find out who you were. As soon as I saw Fairlee arrive I phoned you to come back. I knew this was the time for a showdown.

FRAZER strokes the back of his neck.

FRAZER: It was a showdown, all right!

RICHARDS: (*Smiling*) By the way, here's your camera, Frazer. I meant to bring it the other day but forgot all about it.

FRAZER: Thank you.

FRAZER looks at the case RICHARDS hands him, obviously a shade puzzled. He takes the camera out of the case and examines it.

RICHARDS: (*Looking at FRAZER*) What's wrong, Frazer?

FRAZER: This isn't my camera …

ROSS: Not yours? But that's the one you …

ROSS stops speaking. He picks up the other camera and puts it in front of FRAZER.

ROSS: What about this one?

FRAZER: Yes – this is mine all right.

RICHARDS: Then that explains the switching of the films.

FRAZER: What do you mean?

ROSS: That's the camera we found by Cordwell's body. Yours.

FRAZER: But why should Cordwell want to exchange his camera for mine?

ROSS: I don't think he did. The film he had in his camera – the one of Leo Salinger, being knocked down – was far more valuable to a blackmailer than your film of Barbara Day. It's my bet the switch was never intended; it was accidental.

FRAZER: Accidental? You mean I picked up his camera by mistake.

RICHARDS: (*Indicating*) Yes. The cases are almost identical.

FRAZER: Wait a minute! Do you know, I believe you're right. The only time I met him – at the café in Amsterdam – he had his camera with him. (*Thoughtfully*) And if I remember rightly he put it on the floor to make more room on the table … My camera was on the floor, too, I was sitting next to him. (*Looking at ROSS*) I remember it now – he said he'd just had his camera returned by the police. It had been stolen from his hotel on a previous visit, about a month before.

ROSS: Yes, that's right.

FRAZER: Well, I'm damned!

ROSS: (*Smiling*) Yes, well there you are. (*He rises*) I'm grateful to you, Frazer. You've made a good job of this assignment.

FRAZER: Well – I'm glad it turned out the way it did; about Salinger, I mean.

ROSS: Yes. (*He looks at FRAZER*) I suppose you think I was unduly sentimental. What the hell did it matter whether Salinger was innocent or guilty? The man was dead. Well – he was on my staff, so it did matter – to me, at any rate. (*He holds out his hand*) I'll be in touch with you again, Frazer.

FRAZER: You've no idea when that's likely to be?

ROSS: No, I'm afraid I haven't. Not at the moment. But don't stray too far afield. And let Hobson know where to get hold of you.

RICHARDS: You can give me a lift, Frazer. I'm going your way.

FRAZER: I'm afraid I walked here.

RICHARDS: (*Smiling*) Then I'll give you a lift.

FRAZER goes out with RICHARDS.

ROSS sits at his desk and studies one of the many documents in front of him.

CUT TO: A Busy Street in the West End of London. Day.

A taxi pulls up and FRAZER gets out. RICHARDS remains in the taxi and is looking at FRAZER through the open window.

FRAZER: Goodbye, Richards! Take care of yourself. Don't do anything I wouldn't do.

RICHARDS: Same to you, Frazer. And keep out of coffee bars.

FRAZER looks at RICHARDS for a moment, a flicker of sadness in his expression, then he smiles and with a friendly wave walks away.

THE END

Press Pack

Press cuttings about Tim Frazer and the Salinger Affair ...

Mr Francis Durbridge has created enormous curiosity on many occasions but I doubt whether he has ever caused more bewilderment than with the present Tim Frazer episode. Everyone seems to be asking "Who is Ericson?" I am sorry I can't tell them for I don't know and not going to guess as far as Mr Durbridge is concerned.

Nottingham Evening News

Tortuous Torture (contains spoilers)
Isn't the Tim Frazer serial the most maddening you ever watched? Everything, it seems, contributes so subtly towards the mounting climax. Twenty-nine minutes it takes to work you into the state of receptiveness where you are perched crazily on the edge of the chair breathing through your mouth, noting every gesture, following every look, examining every pause for the key to the whole fascinating muddle.

Then, just as the metronome is ticking horribly away, or the coshed Dutchman is on the point of making some weird disclosure, or Tim notices suddenly that he is being menaced by some silent gunman (just out of the picture), there is that frustrating music, the whole thing disappears and the smug little announcer, who had probably seen the whole thing through privately, tells you to look in again next week.

The tragedy is that, after a week, the impact is lost completely – though at the end of another twenty-nine minutes, the thing has happened again, and the thought of the 168 hours between then and 8.15 next Tuesday is too much torture.

The acting and production in this series are quite superb. Does Tim Frazer model his technique on film star Dirk

Bogarde? Certainly he has the same magnetic style. Plot and dialogue are skilfully contrived and, even when the pressure is off a little and Tim is moving from one scene of intrigue to another, there is always that delicious XK 150 to lick one's lips over, and think about saving up for.

Who is it with the gun d'you think? Tim's girlfriend? Her ex-fiancé? It's the craziest kind of torture …

Paisley Daily Express

At Last We'll Find Out Whodunnit by Fred Coke

The arch-criminal of the BBC's serial *The World of Tim Frazer* is due for unmasking this week. And the nation becomes divided between those who "knew it all the time" and those who were led up the garden path to bark up the wrong tree after a red herring – an athletic poser which Mr Francis Durbridge is adept at setting for his viewers.

The third and final section of this 18-part serial begins on Tuesday as the second section ends.

My only criticism of this new technique of winding up one mystery and starting another half-way through an instalment is that we lose that period of reflection which I think must follow all tv whodunnits.

The period for a mental re-shuffle of events; the inquest to decide if the author has been cheating – though Durbridge never does – is essential I believe.

Jack Hedley, whose Tim Frazer is the best tv sleuth we've got while *Maigret* takes a rest, has a personal problem.

Why is it, he wants to know, that millions of viewers to whom his dark, handsome features have become as familiar as the town hall clock never recognise him, as the man of many previous tv successes?

He had leading parts in twenty major tv plays, including *No Trams to Lime Street, Mine Own Executioner, The Small*

Back Room, Four Men In A Dosshouse, The Protest and *The Darkness Outside.*

"But everybody thinks I'm a new boy," he complains.

Even at auditions directors tell him: "We want you to play in the style of that young man in such-and-such a play." Then he has to tell them: "But I was that young man."

I told Mr Hedley that I hadn't yet seen him smile on tv, except in a cynical kind of way, and that perhaps viewers have a shorter memory for the glowering countenance.

He countered with a letter signed by eighteen boarding-school girls just back from holidays: "We are not allowed to watch Tim Frazer any more so please let us have a picture for our dormitory."

POSTSCRIPT CLUE: Who is the off-screen person Tim turned to in the last second of last week's instalment to say: "I didn't know you carried a gun"?

The *Radio Times* "cast in order of appearance" gives the game away. Next, after Tim, is Arthur Fairlee, sick fiancé of Barbara Day, herself high in the list of suspects.

Is Fairlee the master crook? Or is this Durbridge's reddest herring?

Reynolds News

As I Saw It
Once again Francis Durbridge, the wizard of mystery and intrigue, has done his stuff for the BBC. Another "Adventure of Tim Frazer" has been tied up, and before the viewer could pause to think about it the cunning author had pitched him in at the deep end of another teaser.

Now it is up to the cast and the producer, and if Tim Frazer is to achieve the fame and permanence of Mr Durbridge's celebrated Paul Temple there has got to be a change.

Unlike Temple, Frazer can be heard and seen, and it might be a big help to his future career if occasionally he looked happy in the work he is doing for the mysterious Mr Ross.

Wolverhampton Express and Star

Telecrit (contains spoilers)

So now we know. "Ericson," mystery mastermind behind diamond smuggling in the BBC's *The World of Tim Frazer* last night turned out to be the beautiful Barbara Day after all.

This did not surprise me, for two reasons. First, she was obviously concerned in the racket – in an early episode, she received a phone call which made it clear she was familiar with the name of Ericson ... although she later denied all knowledge of it.

Secondly – and far more important – had she emerged from the story innocent, Tim would have found himself decidedly romantically involved with her. All that would be against all the rules of this type of serial.

Make no mistake about it, whatever "It" is, Jack Hedley's Tim Frazer has it. Ask any woman viewer who's watched the series – "just one episode is not enough ... he grows on you," I'm told by one female Frazer fan.

And that brings me to another reason why Barbara Day was practically predestined to be guilty. "Barbara Day?" said another woman viewer, discussing the possibilities of a love-match the other day, "she's nowhere near good enough for him."

Liverpool Echo

My View Last Night by **Bill McGregor** (contains spoilers)

Well, were you right about Tim Frazer's gun-totin' visitor? I hadn't even included Arthur, the sad suitor, in my short list. My money was on Barbara Day, with a saver on Richards, Tim's secret service buddy.

172

I'm delighted to apologise to the suave Richards, but I would have felt cheated if Barbara had turned out to be as innocent as she looked. Like Mr Frazer I thought she was too good to be true!

I criticised Francis Durbridge's technique of overlapping the last two mysteries in this marathon of mystery. This time he succeeded admirably in providing a thrilling pay-off and selling us a "season" for the next lot of strange happenings in Tim's exciting world.

Glasgow Evening Times

With A Bang! (contains spoilers)

Francis Durbridge cheated a bit with the solution to *The Salinger Affair* in the Tim Frazer series on the BBC. Here we had been picking our fancies among the suspects. Then came the denouement and we found they were all in it together. Not just playing the mystery game; but before we had time to protest Tim had shot off on another case, with the kind of characters and situations which have kept us happy to start guessing again. Good fun, good viewing.

Manchester Evening News

How I Saw It Last Night *by* **Neville Randall** (contains spoilers)

The eight and a half million faithful fans of BBC's Tim Frazer satisfied six weeks of curiosity in six minutes last night.

His second adventure had a swift, smooth, taut climax that had me guessing right to the end. Did you guess that the master crook might be Barbara Day, who has spent the last six weeks posing as a very attractive heroine?

There was no breathing space for the fans. True to the new technique of giving the captive millions no chance of escape, Frazer, in a new car, was off on a new investigation.

He is out to solve the murder of another MI5 agent in Wales.

And before he had finished unpacking, he had tumbled on a clue which made sure that I'll be watching next Tuesday.

Without aiming too high, Francis Durbridge is setting a new standard in serial thrillers.

Daily Sketch

Who Is This Man Tim Frazer? by **Alan Morris**

Who is this man Tim Frazer? That is the question millions of televiewers ask every Tuesday as they watch Frazer tracking down the villain in Francis Durbridge's serial about this intrepid undercover agent.

For Jack Hedley, the man who plays Frazer with such outstanding success, was virtually an "unknown" before the series began.

When Hedley, a Londoner, born on October 28 1929, was invalided from the navy in 1953, his one solid qualification was a knowledge of judo, picked up in Japan.

He tried an advertising agency for two years, but his somewhat shy, solitary nature found the atmosphere uncongenial.

Then, strolling along Gower Street one day, he noticed the Royal Academy of Dramatic Art. The name seemed faintly associated with opera, of which Hedley is a fan, so he walked in impulsively.

A few minutes later he was registered as a student.

He became something of a theatrical phenomenon when on the same day he left R.A.D.A. three years ago, he received his first job. He has been working ever since.

After spells in repertory, at the Glasgow Citizens' Theatre, in a West End play with Alastair Sim, in *Cone of Silence* and *Room At The Top* films, and several powerful roles in ITV plays he can afford a four-roomed Mayfair flat, a white sports car, and breakfast in a Park Lane hotel.

At 30 he does mean to afford a wife, although many of his weekly 400 fan letters come from women intrigued by that easy, sophisticated air with its underlying hint of menace.

"I have to play Tim Frazer poker-faced," Hedley said. "If I expressed half the emotions of a fellow in his scrapes I'd be a mental wreck.

"Anyhow, I took the part to escape from a succession of schizophrenics, alcoholics, and assorted bums. I wanted to see me for a change.

"My eight years in the regular Navy, including spells in Malaya and Korea, have helped," Hedley added.

"Self-discipline is vital to an actor, especially on a project like this which can be a form of perpetual motion worse than repertory. The Navy taught me how to keep things going."

He is what is known among actors as "a quick study." Within minutes, his photographic memory stores away a couple of foolscap pages of dialogue.

Practice in *The World of Tim Frazer* has improved the time. So his next task is a theatre drama. *Nobody But Us Chickens* will be no trouble.

For all of his bachelor-gay veneer and speedy success, Hedley thinks deeply about drama. He has a new conception of Claudius in *Hamlet*, seeing him as a sympathetic, although mysterious character.

He also yearns to play the mixed-up commissar of Arthur Koestler's *Darkness At Noon*.

Will *The World of Tim Frazer* return? If so, Hedley doubts he would be in it. "Another round could be dangerous for me," he said. In a professional sense of course …